FACE VALUE

A LAURA DI PALMA MYSTERY

LIA MATERA

S I M O N & S C H U S T E R

NEW YORK LONDON TORONTO SYDNEY TOKYO SINGAPORE

SIMON & SCHUSTER
Rockefeller Center
1230 Avenue of the Americas
New York, New York 10020

SIMON & SCHUSTER and colophon are registered trademarks
of Simon & Schuster Inc.

Designed by Pei Loi Koay
Manufactured in the United States of America

1 3 5 7 9 10 8 6 4 2

Library of Congress Cataloging-in-Publication Data
Matera, Lia.
Face value: a Laura DiPalma mystery/Lia Matera.
p. cm.
1. DiPalma, Laura (Fictitious character)—Fiction. 2. Women
lawyers—California—San Francisco—Fiction. 3. San Francisco
PS 3563.A83537F3   1994
813'.54—dc20   93–27194
CIP
ISBN 0-671-74197-7

To Nina Martin and Susan Kostal,

for ideas without advice;

and to Bob Irvine,

for advice with a punch line.

1

I WATCHED Steve Sayres walk into my office-warming party. Maybe he thought he was obliged, as senior partner of the firm I'd recently worked for, to pretend to wish me well. Maybe the sentiment was even sincere; after all, he'd gotten what he wanted. He'd turned my mentor, Doron White, against me. He'd gotten me fired a few months before my partnership vote.

Sayres looked around, a smile curling his lips. The Law Offices of Laura Di Palma were on a half-empty floor of a renovated box. I shared a waiting room and two secretaries with a five-person public-interest law firm whose partners were long-ago radicals and whose associates did just enough workers' comp to keep solvent.

My office, across the hall from theirs, was large but ugly, with industrial carpets and leased wood veneer furniture. It had a view of traffic creeping toward the freeway from Market Street. It was many blocks from the financial-district suites White, Sayres & Speck occupied.

My conference table and desk were spread with trays of cheese and cold cuts and crudités; nothing fancy, nothing catered. The lawyers from across the hall were drinking so-so wine with good humor. They seemed pleased to have me as a neighbor.

They doubtless approved of my last client. Dan Crosetti had been a bellwether activist accused of shooting his best friend, who'd turned out to be an undercover FBI agent. I'd lost my job over that case.

Sayres had gone to Doron White, founding partner, previously my ally, and made his argument: I was doing pro bono work without the firm's consent; Crosetti's controversial politics might offend our corporate clients; and I had again placed the firm under the jeweler's eye of publicity.

Doron had agreed.

I'd made the firm a lot of money. I'd made the firm famous. But all it took was one refusal to back down and I was out the door.

I'd been forced to choose between what mattered and what looked good. I'd chosen not to become Steven Sayres.

Crossing my unimpressive new office, Sayres wore his smugness like an expensive coat. He was tall and stylishly fit, his emaciated body pumped with stringy muscle. His face was lightly tanned, with lines of harried ill temper etched around his eyes and into his forehead. His graying hair showed comb lines, as if he'd just left the sauna. His suit looked custom-made, his usual dark blue with a wild print tie now that no other kind would do.

"Hello, Laura." He stopped farther from me than was strictly polite. I was glad.

"Steve." I kept my tone friendly, but I didn't extend my hand.

"I wondered if you'd open your own office. Frankly"—he glanced at my relatively ill-dressed neighbors, making lunch of cheese and cold cuts—"I couldn't have given you much of a reference if you'd tried to join one of the big firms here."

I felt a smile chill my face. "A reference from you would have been superfluous, Steve. Everyone here knows me."

"That's right." He slid his hand into his suit pocket. "And everyone here knows how Doron died."

Doron White had suffered a series of anginas that severely damaged his heart. A late-night encounter with a friend of Crosetti's— an encounter in my then-office—had triggered Doron's final and fatal heart attack.

A group of beautifully outfitted people stepped into the room. They were White, Sayres clients, formerly my clients—bank vice presidents, mostly. One, in-house counsel for Graystone Federal, waved at me before smoothing her Lauren Bacall hair. The others looked around, showing their surprise. No expensive paintings here, no tree-sized arrangements of exotic flowers.

I watched Steve. A hot redness spread up his neck and over the slack skin of his jaw. Without motion or overt distress, he'd flamed into a fury. That's how it had begun with Doron, a sudden flush betraying his anger.

The bank clients were upon us now, hand-shaking and well-wishing, smiling at Steve to show they approved of his magnanimous visit. Of course he'd known they'd come; of course he'd had to come, too. If I let him, he'd position himself as Daddy, looking in on his little girl. He'd minimize me because he hadn't been able to sabotage me.

"Steve was just blaming me for Doron's death," I said. "And because Doron and I were close, and I resent it, I'm about to ask Steve to leave."

Steve's face drained of color. Behind me, conversations stopped. Two of Steve's clients stepped back, as if my honesty might sully them.

"I don't work for you anymore, Steve. I don't have to play this game. If you want to insult me, do it out loud for everyone to hear. Don't stand here looking like Lord Bountiful while you complain in my ear you didn't get a chance to blackball me."

He looked at his clients, formerly my clients. His brows were pinched into a mask of pitying chagrin. He used that face in court whenever he could. The clients had seen it there. But they had their own versions of it. I was the rule-breaker here.

That's why I was on my own in an office unfashionably south of Market. That's what Dan Crosetti had done for me. I blessed him silently as I said, "I asked you to leave. Play cute with your clients somewhere else."

"Well"—a bank client turned the word into a hearty sigh—"actually, Steve, if you'll let me walk you back, I should be moving on."

Steve continued looking sad and paternal. "Let me buy you lunch, Bill. Margaret, Harry, can you join us?"

I took Harry's hand and shook it. Did the same to Margaret's. "Thank you so much for coming," I said. "It was good to see you."

Margaret stared at me, openmouthed. Bill put his hand on Steve's arm. "Let's try the new place around the corner. Maybe they can still seat four without a reservation."

Only Margaret seemed to hesitate, her skull-thin face crimped into a silent *But* . . . She finally joined the chorus of good-byes and good-lucks.

I watched two major banks and a mortgage brokerage walk out my door. They would spread the word, no doubt: Laura Di Palma was being hysterical. Maybe radical. She'd been gone almost ten months, no one was sure where, not practicing law, having some kind of mid-life crisis, probably. She hadn't gone back to big-firm practice; she'd gone solo—and not even at a good address.

I turned to join the left-wing lawyers from across the hall. My practice, assuming I developed one in time to pay my lease and meet my small payroll, would not cut into Steve Sayres's.

That was fine with me.

"You look like you could use a glass of wine. White or red?" Dennis Hyerdahl, known for some colorful conspiracy theories, circa 1968, handed me a plastic glass.

"White."

Hyerdahl, slacks too low and tie too short over his middle-aged belly, poured the wine. One of the firm's associates, a small blonde in a linty black suit, grinned.

"We've been looking forward to meeting you, to tell the truth." Pat Frankel's voice retained a hint of Larchmont, and her face was tanned almost to premature leatheriness. A sailor, probably. A preppy who'd taken a sharp turn left. "We heard you could be pretty, um, blunt."

I'd gotten a lot of press defending a man who'd assassinated two United States senators. In the process of getting him acquitted, I'd developed a reputation for being aggressive. I supposed that's what she meant.

I took a quick swallow. "In my business dealings. When it's appropriate."

Hyerdahl laughed. "Blunt, I love it. God, yes, give me blunt."

Frankel elbowed him. "Diplomacy is hardly your problem."

"Oh, Ms. Tactful here. Did I not hear you call your client a whiner this morning? Hmmm? Patricia?"

A joking wince. "Her organization. Besides, she's not my client."

"Anymore, ha-ha." He seemed to have no desire to follow up, to check up. If I'd had a boss like that, I wouldn't be here now.

"You know, Laura"—Frankel's eyes shined a manic blue—"I should refer her to you. If you do First Amendment stuff."

"Yes." I do anything that pays the rent, right now. Anything that underwrites malpractice premiums and my share of Hyerdahl's common-area expenses, anything that pays for use of his law library and secretaries, his Xerox machines and voice mail. Even on the cheap, opening a practice had depleted my savings and exhausted my credit.

"She actually has an interesting case." Frankel leaned against the desk, coattails nudging the Brie. "I just got a little impatient with her. She's part of a group I did some pro bono work for, but eons ago. She's still back in the Call-Me-*Ms*.-Tibbs era of feminism, as if we haven't moved way beyond— No, I should shut up and refer her to you; let you make up your own mind. I've definitely got baggage on this one."

In commercial practice, one did not acquire baggage. It was impossible to care that much about a bank.

I looked around my new office. It wasn't the dramatic array of red leathers and accent pieces my last office had been. It lacked a view of flower vendors and street quartets and scrubbed stone highrises. But these people were across the hall now, not Steve Sayres. And I chose my own cases.

There were things I missed too much to think about. But those were the early days under Doron's wing, when I had been thrilled with the status and the responsibility. It had gone inalterably sour. That had happened to a lot of lawyers, except they remained in their purgatory of overwork and underappreciation.

Thank you, Dan Crosetti.

MY WINDOWS and door were open to create a breeze. I poured sweating curls of cheese into a trash bag and brushed crumbs off the desktop. I was watching a videotape on a television hidden in a corner cabinet. It was a compilation of news footage about the two cases that had put me on the map. It had arrived gift-wrapped with a "Congratulations on Your New Job" greeting card. The card was bare of salutation or comment and was signed simply "Aunt Diana." I was sure she hadn't made the tape herself. "Uncle" Henry (my father's second cousin, as close to him as a brother) had probably forgotten it with his post-divorce leavings.

Though Diana would ordinarily have loved gloating about a famous relative, she loathed me. She couldn't be overt about it—I added to her stature, after all; hence, a gift not of her making and a merely civil card.

I tossed the card into the garbage. She could have added a line about her son.

Hal and I had grown up in mutual dislike and conflict. When we fell in love decades later, we discussed little; any subject might become a mine field of old jealousies and irritations. We spent four hard years together. Three months ago he left; just gave up and left. Funny I could miss him so much and yet find life without him a relief.

I'd traced him to Alaska, to an artsy little nowhere called Homer. Diana might have let me know whether the family had heard from him.

On my television screen, I explained a defense strategy to reporters who'd consistently mis-characterized it.

The image in the box didn't match the one in my mirror. The mirror gave me back a slim woman, obviously of Italian descent: nose a little large, lips full, Joan Crawford brows over green eyes, few white hairs among the brown. Yet the Dorian Gray on my television looked disconcertingly heavier, older, unflatteringly strident under her ice. I listened to my explanation of the "television syndrome" defense: that television creates a reality more powerful than personal experience. I watched, measuring the truth of my argument by the battering my self-image was taking.

A voice interrupted. "Laura? I took a chance on finding you in."

"Margaret." I was surprised to see Graystone Federal's in-house counsel at my door. She'd registered in my consciousness this morning only as part of a group I'd written off.

"Do you have time right now?" Her gaunt face seemed unnaturally tight. Not a face lift? She was about forty, about my age; surely she was too young? She blinked rapidly, anchoring a smooth wave of hair behind her ear.

"Please come in." I clicked off the television, letting the videotape wind on. I'd seen enough.

I motioned Margaret into a cheap chair. There were round aluminum trays on my desk, bare of their Safeway cold cuts. I placed them on the floor. "Is this social? Or a bank problem?"

I tried not to get my hopes up. She probably couldn't hire co-counsel without a vice president's approval. And Graystone's VP, as far as I knew, was a White, Sayres loyalist.

"It's a personal problem." She was seated now, as long and flat as a ribbon in the hard fabric chair. With her belted knit dress and sleek forties hair, she looked like a fragile film-noir heroine. I re-

membered her as having an edge-of-the-chair, health-club vitality.
Her languidness surprised me.

"Tell me about it." I sat back, expecting to hear about a botched
lease or a minor car accident.

"For the record"—she fixed me with bright eyes—"I'd like to hire
you. I'd like you to be my lawyer."

For the record: telling me the lawyer-client privilege was kicking
in.

"My fee is ten percent lower than what I billed at White, Sayres.
Is that all right?"

"Yes."

"I'll have an agreement typed up and sent to you. This consul-
tation is on me."

"Thank you." There was a quality in her look that startled me. I
didn't know how to read it. Fear? Shame? "I've been walking around
with this for days, not knowing who to contact. I can't imagine going to any of the firms I know. I know so many people."

She knew me. Why was I different?

"The rumor is you went off to Seattle or someplace, Laura. Is
that right?"

"Northern California. Up near the Oregon border."

"And you didn't practice at all?"

"My . . . cousin was sick. I stayed with him." It wasn't a lie, but
it came nowhere near the truth. Hal had been battling right-side
weakness from a Vietnam War injury, but that's not what we'd hoped
to heal, up there.

"And you didn't go back to White. I guess I need to think you've
been going through this lawyer thing like the rest of us."

"Lawyer thing?"

"Did you see in *California Lawyer* that seventy percent of the
lawyers they polled hate their careers and want to leave?"

"No. I've been out of the loop."

"You're lucky. I haven't had a real vacation in seven years. If Graystone had its way, I'd do nothing but work. Work and work out—all the firms offer gym memberships now. So we'll look good, look healthy; so the stress won't show. Maybe outsiders can't tell. But it's clear to all of us, isn't it?"

I was a little off balance. "That lawyers aren't happy?"

"We've given away all our free time for as long as we can re-member—all the things we cared about: family life, political com-mitment, travel, spirituality. We put all that energy into work. And working out so we'll be fit enough to work so much. You know what I mean?"

Her voice spiraled in pitch. This was obviously a problem she was far from solving.

"There really is a kind of seven-year itch in this profession, Laura, don't you think? About the time we make partner we realize we blew off all the stuff that really mattered to us. I know at least a dozen lawyers who couldn't stand it anymore, who ran off to climb some mountain in Nepal or up and became roofers or something."

"Those people come back. Usually to the same firm for less money."

"I know. I know that. That was part of it. I've known for a long time I was unhappy, but I didn't want to do a mid-life-crisis kind of thing. I didn't want a consolation prize—a red Beamer or a sailboat or a trip. I wanted something real."

I didn't like the sound of that. It's easy to think the things you don't have are more "real" than the things you do. Some are; most aren't. I'd found that out the hard way with Hal.

She continued, "I was raised a Lutheran. They always told us, 'work hard and judge not.' But 'judge not' was just an aphorism on a plaque. What they really meant was 'be like us because we're good.' You weren't supposed to think or question beyond that. It's perfect training for being a lawyer: work and conform; nonconformity is sin."

Welcome to mass culture. But then, I guess ideas are made profound by their relevance to your situation. This had nothing to do with me.

"I found a teacher, a real spiritual mother. Master, I mean." She lost her look of dull enervation. Her cheeks suffused with color.

"A master?" Growing up under Hal's mother's thumb, I'd longed for the day I could be free. I couldn't conceive of wanting a master.

"I can tell that offends you."

"No."

"You can be honest, Laura."

Not if it meant being personal. "You found a master," I prompted.

"He's wonderful. Totally unlike anyone else. I heard about him through a case I had. One of our debtors was a devotee. I started hanging out with the group, and suddenly it was like I was back in college. All-night conversations, brilliant people discussing the philosophy of science and the nature of reality." She clenched her fists and stared at them. "This part's hard. I don't want to go into the philosophy and all that. Not that it isn't up-and-up—it's very scientific; he's a physicist, quantum physics, on the cutting edge of computers and holographic-universe stuff. But that's just detail."

I was glad my client was a lawyer. I didn't have to sift chaff.

"In terms of why I'm here"—she reddened, looked increasingly uncomfortable—"we got into exploring various aspects of ourselves—'energies,' Brother Mike calls them. Especially negative energies, you know, things we get hung up on that become insidious, that become the basis for actions that should be independent of them."

I waited. "Go on."

"A lot of us had . . . problems involving sexuality."

I hoped I wasn't going to hear tales of orgies and forced sex. I hoped I wasn't going to hear about yet another guru with Rolls Royces and love slaves.

"Brother is very scientifically advanced. He believes technology is our window to the psycho-physical universe." She blinked at me, biting her lower lip. "So everything we did in terms of exploring our sexual problems we, um, did on videotape. He reimages the film on his computer."

"*Reimages*? As in 'to image again'?"

"That's right. He changes it using graphics and animation programs. It's very powerful. He changes it in ways that are absolutely knockout in terms of showing us things about ourselves. It's astounding, really."

"What does he do? Put different heads on your bodies or something?"

"Nothing that overt. It's more changing our expressions, imaging-in our auras—they're like magnetic fields—showing their actions and interactions."

I looked at the well-dressed bank lawyer sitting across from me. I couldn't believe what I was hearing. Sex videos with reimaged auras. And this was her idea of "real."

"I gather some sort of problem developed?"

She shrank back into the chair. "He's released them."

"The videos?"

"Yes. For distribution. Someone I know saw them at a video rental place. In the adult room. I guess they had a shelf labeled 'Amateur,' and there they were. I went and looked. There's a dozen of them. I rented one. I'm on it."

"Recognizably? Or did the reimaging change you?"

"I think I'm recognizable. I think my facial expressions"—her cheeks looked scalded—"might have been changed, but I can't be sure."

"Has he changed other people's expressions?"

"I think so. But it's such an intense experience. My memories of it are subjective. And the tapes he showed us"—her hands clutched the wool on her lap—"they had a point. The reimaging revealed things about us. Whereas the tape I rented was just sex. Even the auras are gone."

"Does he narrate the tapes? Is there a plot?"

She shook her head. "The one I saw was just our session."

"Did you sign any kind of release?"

"Yes. But I never thought Brother was going to distribute the tapes. I thought the release was a formality. There are quite a few lawyers in the group—I assumed they'd advised him to be cautious, that they were protecting him. I didn't think twice about it."

People assume lawyers are more careful than others about signing contracts. I've never found that to be the case.

"Do you have a copy?"

"Not with me. I don't even know . . ."

"If you want to enjoin distribution of the tapes? Seek money damages?"

"I guess I want to know what my options are. I guess I'm afraid to talk to Brother. He always makes sense to me, really speaks to me. You know, on a deeper level. And I guess I'm afraid of that. I'd like someone who doesn't feel that way about him to find out why he's doing this. Because I know he'll make me think was a good thing for him to do."

"And you don't feel that way now. You feel betrayed."

She sat very still. "Brother wouldn't betray me."

But he would distribute pornographic videos of you. "Tell me the name of the video rental store, and fax me a copy of the release later today. I'll get back to you tomorrow with a report on what I saw on the videos and an opinion of the release. Then we'll decide what you want me to say to this Brother. How would that be?"

Her face crumpled. "This is very difficult for me."

"If you'll authorize the expense, I'd like to associate-in a private detective so we can get a little background information on the guru and on the extent of the video distribution. It could make a difference in terms of how you want to approach this. Information is strength."

"I don't want a battle, Laura."

"You've been a bank lawyer long enough to know the stronger your position, the less likely you are to have to fight."

"Unless it turns into an ego thing."

"True. But you don't want that to happen. And I want what you want."

She looked at me. She knew my track record. She also knew my weakness. There were times I could have settled things more quickly by being less aggressive.

"I'll try to be careful not to screw up your spiritual relationship. But my main objective will be to get what you decide you want. If that's an injunction against distribution, I'll make that my priority. That's why you need a lawyer. You've got a master-devotee relationship with this person. You start out from a position of supplication, so you know you're not going to put your best interests first. Not without objective advice."

"The videos are at that place on Twenty-fourth near Army. I'll fax the release to you. And if you really think a private detective is a good idea, I guess go ahead."

"I'm sure it's a good idea." I knew whom I would contact. I hoped he'd return my call, this time.

"The other thing I wanted to tell you . . ." It was closer to a question than a statement. "One of the main people that—I don't know how to put this—*sexualized*, I guess, is the best word . . . The main person who sort of got us all into this, who got Brother into the sexual aspects. You know, who stirred us up sexually so that Brother ended up having to help us get through some of our stuff . . ." She clasped and unclasped her hands, speaking to the wall behind me. "I've had a relationship with her."

"A relationship? Of what nature?"

She told the spot behind me. "Romantic."

"Okay. Is she also in the tapes?"

"Yes."

"Have you talked to her? Do you know how she feels about the distribution?"

"I think . . . I'm afraid . . ." Margaret finally met my eye. "I think distributing the tapes might have been Arabella's idea."

"Does that complicate things for you? Are you still having a relationship? Are you afraid this is going to jeopardize it?"

"Arabella is, um, a sex worker. So, um, she has a lot of relationships."

"A sex worker? Is she a prostitute?"

"She's an exotic dancer. At The Back Door."

I nodded. A sex club with a reputation for being hipper than the blinking-nipples-on-billboards places on Broadway.

"You say your relationship was romantic. Does that mean more than sexual?"

"Yes." Her voice was husky.

"When you say she has a lot of relationships, do you mean romantic or just sexual?"

"Both. She's very attractive on many levels. And not monogamous. And I don't—" She was getting upset, short of breath. "I don't want to lose her. I don't want to lose Brother, either."

"But you don't want to be recognizably featured on videos made available to the public. I'll do my best." I wondered if I should offer her a tissue or some wine. I wondered if I should pat her shoulder.

Corporate practice had been easy in that regard. My two criminal cases had presented more emotional complications than all my corporate cases combined.

I'd never been good at dealing with emotion, mine or anyone else's.

I was relieved when Margaret stood to leave. She fumbled in her briefcase for a moment, pulling out a flier.

It was triple-folded blue paper. One side read FIGHT CENSORSHIP. The words jostled a collage of faces and bodies, some famous, many nude.

"Arabella's probably going to perform at this benefit. She starts work right afterward." Margaret handed me the flier without looking at me. "The Back Door's giving up its main room for a couple of hours. If you need to speak to her or just want to see her. Maybe Brother's going to be there, I don't know. It's tomorrow night. I probably won't go."

"Thank you." I took the flier. "I'll speak to you again before then. I may want to go. It'll depend on what's on the tapes, and what you decide you'd like me to do."

She seemed broken, without will. I hoped it was a result of stress and confusion. I hoped it didn't go deeper; I hoped this guru hadn't shaken her confidence.

She was in-house counsel for a bank, after all. She couldn't afford to get too docile.

She looked me in the eye. "It's tearing the lesbian community apart, did you know that?"

"Your guru?"

She pointed to the pamphlet. "That. You'll see, if you go."

She hurried out of my office.

I opened the pamphlet. "Reclaim sexuality! Reclaim erotica! Reclaim America!" it read. "Join us in speaking out against censorship. Join us for a very special show at The Back Door Theater."

Tearing the lesbian community apart? I wondered what she meant.

I noticed my hand was shaking. But that had nothing to do with Margaret's problem. It had to do with the call I was about to make.

"SANDY?" I COULDN'T keep the edge out of my voice. The last time we talked, we quarreled. Sander Arkelett, private detective for White, Sayres, among others, had been my lover for a while. I'd left him for Hal; he'd been a good sport, considering. But three months ago, an intense attraction to another man showed me my feelings for Hal had reverted to familial. And Sandy hadn't liked Ted McGuin, hadn't liked it that Ted was younger, less educated, part of a different world; he'd been downright insulting about it, in fact. He'd acted like my father, with his disapproval and dire warnings.

I hadn't spoken to Sandy since I'd returned to San Francisco. I'd called him. I'd left messages. But he hadn't phoned back. Until now, my reaction had been, well then, the hell with you.

"It's Laura." This was the first time I'd called his work number. I guess I'd known I could reach him there.

I tried to put the resentment away.

"Sandy, God damn it. Say something."

A slow exhalation. "Howdy."

Still coming on like a laid-back cowboy, a just-folks Gary Cooper.

"You knew I was back." I left you enough messages.

"Yuh. Office down in SoMa, I hear."

"Only a little south of Market."

"Least you're back in business. I was glad to learn."

Then why didn't you return my calls, you sanctimonious, paternalistic son of a bitch? "That's why I'm calling. I'd like to hire you."

"Go on."

"There's a guru here in town—I don't even have his full name yet. His followers call him Brother."

A brief silence. "I know about him."

"How?"

"Previous investigation."

He couldn't tell me about the investigation, but maybe he could tell me what he'd learned about Brother. That would save my client money; keep my fee low and make me look good.

"I have a client who's involved with him. I need background on him. Unless you have a conflict."

"Depends who your client is. What the problem is."

"Her name is Margaret Lenin. She did some kind of sex-therapy sessions with him. She let him videotape them. Now the tapes are available in at least one video rental place."

"Smooth move. She suing?"

"She doesn't know what she wants to do. I haven't seen the release she signed, and I don't know what his plans are in terms of distribution of the videos."

"Well." I could hear him breathe into the mouthpiece. "I don't see a conflict on my end. I don't know."

I waited awhile, and then I said, "I'm not with McGuin, but I don't think that should matter. I think you were out of line." I waited a little longer. "I think you were a real shithead."

"That your idea of an olive branch?"

"You could have returned my calls."

"You could have come home with me and taken care of business instead of scratching your itch."

I hung up. Conservative ex-cop, disapproving bastard, treating me like a kid. Worse, like his ex-wife.

When the phone rang a minute later, I knew it was him. I waited for one of the secretaries across the hall to put the call through.

"All right," he said, a little extra Louisiana in his voice. "You want me, you got me."

4

I SAT WITH my back to a wall of unpacked boxes, a tumbler of iced vodka in my hand. My new apartment didn't feel right, didn't feel like me. There was too much architecture in my viewshed, not enough greenery. I missed my old place, stately and fragrant with eucalyptus from the Presidio across the street.

Even my furniture looked shabby now. Hal hadn't bothered to keep the fat white sofas clean, to keep the antique wood unringed. I'd watched it happen, worrying about my yuppie fixation on externals, trying not to care about mere things.

For my sake more than Hal's, I'd allowed my furniture to grow nicked and soiled. I'd walked away from my career and drained my savings. And it hadn't changed either of us, not enough.

I wondered if he was happy in Alaska. He was working on a fishing boat—rigorous enough work to test the right-arm, right-leg weakness that was the legacy of his Vietnam tour. For almost twenty years he'd yoked himself to his denial. Maybe I'd done the same.

After four years of complicated interaction with him—I couldn't call it romance, really—I supposed he'd remain my silent partner for a long time. He was still the one I talked to in my head, the one I showed things to and justified things to. It was, on the whole, unpleasant to support so harsh an inner companion. But maybe that's why I did it.

I poured another glass of vodka and popped a tape into my video-cassette player.

It opened with a light show, a startling montage of spectra fading and blending into each other. It was very sixties, making me expect the usual corny bullshit.

But then, I knew nothing about this guru's philosophy. Maybe it was preferable to most people's; maybe even to mine. I just couldn't imagine substituting someone else's observations for my own. On the other hand, Margaret Lenin was a smart woman; if she was impressed, maybe there was something to be impressed by.

The opening scene was a group of eight adults ranging in age from mid-twenties to mid-forties, by the look of them. They were undressing, quickly and without sidelong glances.

A bored-sounding voice captured everyone's attention. I assumed it belonged to Brother.

"Now let's begin," the voice said, as if for the thousandth time guiding children through *The Charge of the Light Brigade*. "Let's begin with why we're here. We know that reality, as defined by our civilization, is an inadequate guess. It doesn't even explain its own principles of physics. Quantum physics tells us the rules are different for subatomic particles. An electron is a wave when it's not observed and a particle when it is observed. Our perceptions actually, literally change matter—make it real, if you will. So it's no overstatement, no silly tenet of pseudoscience or mystical religion to say that this is a psycho-physical universe. Our perceptions create not only *our* reality, but on the quantum level—which is the basis of all matter—reality itself." A slight pause. "Please make yourselves comfortable."

The devotees dropped to big cushions arranged in a circle on the floor. A number of them kept arms folded across their breasts or hands strategically over their genitals. The camera executed a slow sweep, as if the speaker were pacing, addressing each individual. The effect was cinema verité made folksy by amateurish handling of the video recorder.

"Sexuality is a perfect example," the voice continued. "Our bodies respond to our perceptions and interpretations. We turn ourselves on by selecting stimuli, sometimes of a personal and highly individual nature. But that's not the end of it. We proceed to put our sexuality—our heat, our wanting, our energy—out into the world. We do it so others will respond. Often we do it inadvertently, chagrined to see it push people away like a negative magnetic wave. Just as we see the *effects* of subatomic waves—magnetism, for example, or gravity—and not the waves themselves, we know our sexuality by its effects in the world. We create sexual fields and they in turn create and are changed by interference patterns with other fields, sexual and nonsexual."

I wondered if people renting the video would fast-forward through the capsule philosophy, or if the nakedness of the devotees would hold their interest. The bodies were less perfect than the usual late-night cable images. But they were all reasonably trim and fit—perhaps the out-of-shape had declined to be part of the group.

"You wouldn't be in this room if you weren't powerfully aware of your sexual energy, and powerfully pulled into the energy of the people around you. The interference patterns created by your energies can be transduced into a new understanding, an intuition about the nature of reality and consciousness. You're here to open yourself to it. Change the patterns of habit that inhibit your progress. Make a gesture toward the future. Begin by touching yourself."

I found myself sitting forward, equally rapt and disgusted. Group members exhibited signs of shyness now that action was required of them. Some fidgeted, some sat stone-still. They gave the impression of baby boomers at a seminar suddenly discovering they were naked. How far were they going to go to please this laconic voice?

They had apparently been coached. After the first tense moment, they lay back on their cushions. They began tentatively stroking themselves.

The camera began revolving around the circle, focusing on genitals. Though they lacked the shaved grooming seen in girlie magazines, they didn't reflect the variety found in locker rooms, either.

Soon the tape urged the devotees to "play," and they reached under their cushions for an array of sex toys, most of which were far outside my experience. I moved closer to the screen.

As the tape wound on, I was struck by two things. One was the film quality. Shot with a video camera, it didn't have the professional distance of 35 millimeter. It was as cozy as a home movie, and that was disconcerting, as if a family picnic had swerved into debauchery. On the other hand, the color was extraordinary, more vivid and crisper than the usual faded home video.

The other thing I noticed was that not everyone in the group was aroused. Six of the eight apparently were. They watched the others, arched their backs, reached out for one another, licked their lips for camera close-ups.

But two women seemed to be in trouble. One turned away from the camera. What could be seen of her face betrayed no fear or pain, but the way she held herself disturbed me. Sometimes she trembled. Insertion seemed difficult.

Another woman looked ecstatic, but the men on either side of her seemed to be holding her down.

The voice on the tape commanded the group to "share the energy, mingle the waves," and suddenly some devotees were stroking and licking others, eliciting embarrassed-sounding cries from them.

What followed was an orgy for some, maybe a gang rape for the others. It was difficult to decide whether the two women had grown more relaxed. They definitely did not try to stop it or to leave. Facially, they seemed to enjoy what they were doing: that might have been a function of their commitment to the philosophy. I hoped it wasn't the result of computer retouching.

This tape, the first in the series, continued to be clumsily amateurish. Attempts to zoom in on coupled organs and questing tongues had produced a headache-inducing blur of limbs in the way. The video lasted thirty-some minutes, probably edited from an hour or two of activity.

I spread the movie boxes on the floor in front of me. The one I'd seen was titled *Orgy of Energy*. Others bore titles like *The Energy of Enslavement, The Energy of Pain, The Energy of the Tantras, Male Energy, The Energy of Women, The Energy of Obedience, The Energy of Narcissism*.

I found, by fast-forwarding through them, that whatever the theme, the format was fairly uniform: Brother's voice preaching a gospel of sexuality coupled with some pretext for exploring a certain kind of "energy."

I was surprised to find so little variety of body type. There were few sags and stretch marks visible, few saddlebags and blemishes. Like other "erotic" films I'd seen, these tracked lowest-common-denominator fantasies featuring people who, for the most part, might have stepped off a television set. They left me feeling as if I'd watched a particularly embarrassing episode of *"The Newlywed Game."* They made me want to distance myself from mass culture, to flee into the artistic refinement of classic novels and old jazz.

In spite of his quantum-physics sermonizing, Brother's videos seemed standard fare.

I could understand Margaret's distress. If the films had been initially reimaged to make a spiritual point, it must be disconcerting to see them repackaged as garden-variety pornography.

It was in the final video of the set, The *Energy of Honest Sex*, that I encountered the image most shocking to me. The focus was on stream-of-consciousness communication during intercourse. One of the participants had been a law-school classmate of mine. She grimaced as a much older man entered her from behind. She told him he repulsed her. She told him she hated it. And she looked as if she meant it.

Others in the group rambled about their fantasies. They seemed to be having a fine time.

I had been watching for Margaret Lenin. I hadn't expected to see anyone else I knew. And because it was the one instance of someone unequivocally not enjoying the act, it seemed ghastly.

I'd expected some version of this feeling when I saw my client. But I didn't see her, not in any of the tapes. I checked the list of available videos against the ones I'd rented. According to my list, I had all of them.

Margaret Lenin had recognized herself on one of these. But I hadn't.

I didn't want to watch them again. Tomorrow, I'd ask her which tape. The title would remind me of the content. I'd review it later.

Right now, I wanted to soak in a tub until I felt clean.

WHEN I REACHED my office the next morning, I already had a phone message from Margaret Lenin. I returned her call.

"Did you see the tapes? Did you see me?" Her voice was tight.

"I fast-forwarded through parts. Which one were you in?" The smell of wine and cheese lingered in my office, mingling with the chemical smell of industrial carpet. Although my door was closed, I could hear the blond lawyer across the hall shouting at someone.

"The first one. *Orgy*."

"I started with that one. I saw the whole thing. But I . . ." I thought about the tape; couldn't believe any of those women had been Margaret. None had seemed so thin, for one thing. "Are you sure you're in that one?"

"Yes. All he did was open my eyes wider. And make my lips a little . . . You really didn't recognize me?"

"No. I thought you said he hadn't reimaged it much."

"Compared to the major stuff he did with the film before we saw it, it was nothing. I didn't even notice he'd done anything the first time I watched it. I guess since I knew it was me . . ."

"I really didn't recognize you." I was ambivalent about asking which woman she'd been. I supposed the tape had made her look heavier; maybe she'd been one of the reluctant two. "I find it hard to believe I wouldn't recognize your hair, at least."

"I don't curl the ends when I'm off work."

"But the changes you describe are so small. Do you think people who've seen your body . . . ?" This was not my ideal conversation.

"Those people wouldn't care. And I don't care about them knowing. I guess what I'm thinking . . . if you really, truly didn't recognize me . . . ."

I waited. If she was dropping the case, she'd do it without help from me.

"Maybe I should just leave it alone, Laura. I was talking to a friend about it last night: I'll have trouble proving damages if nobody's likely to recognize me. And the main thing the judge will think is, why did she bring a lawsuit and call attention to this if she didn't want to be recognized?"

"On the other hand, your image has been used in a commercial pornographic film. You have every right to want to stop distribution." But that was as naive as it was true. "I'm not recommending a lawsuit. I'm just saying you probably have a viable cause of action. Whether it's in your best interests to pursue it, I don't know. Only you can make that decision. I can call you back—"

"No need." Her voice was low with relief. "It doesn't make sense to go on with it. Not if you can't tell it's me. I'm just sorry I wasted your time."

Sorry she'd let an acquaintance into a very private aspect of her life.

"I understand, Margaret. But why don't you take some time to think about it? Maybe watch the tape again and see how you feel."

"No." Her voice said: I need this to be over; I don't want to think about it anymore. "Let's just drop it."

I wondered if she'd return to the group, keep following her guru. I wanted to urge her to buy a new car, take a long trip; find a more usual expression of her dissatisfaction.

"Naturally, bill me for the time you spent watching the tapes."

"Yes. Shall I send my statement to your home address?"

She rattled it off, sounding relieved. No one at work would have to know.

Or so we thought.

I WOULDN'T HAVE canceled my lunch date with Sandy regardless. As it turned out, I had good reason to keep it.

Gretchen Miller, the law-school classmate I'd seen on last night's video, phoned me. She asked me to come by her office. I knew it had something to do with Brother and the videos and Margaret Lenin. It had to.

On the phone, she would only say, "It's about a potential case."

I checked in across the hall before leaving. Hyerdahl's firm was decorated in multi-cultural art. African masks hung beside Latin American tapestries. One wall was covered with a sincere rain-forest mural. It gave the office a toasty earnestness.

I told our shared secretary that I'd be out until afternoon. She grinned. I'd been averaging one phone call a day. She seemed confident in her ability to handle the volume.

As I turned, I nearly collided with Pat Frankel, who was storming into the office. She stopped, looking up at me.

"You've got to take a referral." She scowled, but not, I thought, at me. She ran her fingers through her chin-length hair, brushed off her grape-colored suit.

"From you?"

"Yes. Did you hear a crazy lady in the hall a while ago?"

"I heard you."

A quick laugh. "I meant the referral. I was going to open your door and push her in just to get rid of her. She won't take no for an answer. I argued with her all the way downstairs. She's so high on sanctimony, she acts like the only moral thing for me to do is take her case. God. I'll owe you if you take her. I told her you'd represented Dan Crosetti. That makes you politically correct enough for her."

"This is the person you were telling me about, the one you won't represent because you have baggage?"

"My whiner; that's right. I'm being hideously unfair—she's okay; she just punches my buttons. You want to go out for coffee or something?" She seemed in better humor now, her preppily sunburned face relaxed.

"I have a meeting." I regretted it. For the first time in months, I felt a stirring of sociability. "What's the whiner's name? In case she calls."

"Megan Carter. You don't know her, do you? If she doesn't call you, I'll feel guilty about gratuitously bad-mouthing her."

"No, I don't know her. If she calls, I'll let you know."

"So I can feel safely rid of her." She grinned. "It's good having you across the hall. We have a surplus of weirdos. We'll send some your way."

I hoped she wasn't kidding.

"MS. MILLER WILL see you now," the receptionist told me. She watched me as I rose from a leather couch. "Third door on the left."

I wondered if she knew what we'd be discussing. Did she know she could rent a tape of her boss bending over for a guru?

Gretchen greeted me at her office door.

"Laura." She extended her long hand to be shaken.

She was beautifully dressed in a braid-trimmed emerald suit that hugged her tall, very slender body. Her hair was earlobe-length on one side, moussed into a wave. On the other, it was razored to a near crew cut. It took a long neck and delicate bone structure to carry off the style; on her, it looked smashing.

"How are you, Gretchen?" I asked the question, but I'd already drawn a few conclusions. She worked for a small but respected firm. She was gorgeously groomed, and greeted me without embarrassment. She was okay.

"It's nice to see you again, Laura. I've thought of you several times, thought about giving you a call."

She waved me into a turquoise suede chair. Behind her desk, a floor-to-ceiling window framed a bit of financial-district tower. If she swung her office chair around and craned her neck, she'd have a street view of potted flowers and a landmark black lump sculpture nicknamed "The Banker's Heart." My old office was close by.

Gretchen sat opposite me on a suede love seat, tugging her skirt over her knee. I tried to lose my mental image of her unclothed. If I'd seen her at the health club, I wouldn't dwell on it.

"I'd like to send a case your way, Laura. It involves a man named Michael Hover. He's known as Brother Mike, or just Brother. He's not a traditional guru, but he does have a following; maybe three, four hundred people in this area." There was no trace of a blush on her porcelain, lightly freckled cheeks. But she had to know Margaret Lenin had consulted me.

"I do know about him, Gretchen. You must realize that."

"You mean Margaret. I know she came to you. I also know she decided not to hire you. And I think that's smart: she's really not recognizable. She'd be defeating her own purpose."

"How did you find out about Margaret?"

"She told us." Gretchen looked so elegant, the "us" might have been royal.

"Told your group?"

"Told me and another devotee. Last night. We watched the tape with her. Talked about Mike." I noticed she didn't call him Brother. "She'd never have gone through with suing him, Laura. He'd never give her reason. He'd never have left her recognizable, not if it bothered her."

"He left you recognizable, Gretchen." I felt as if I'd thrown a grenade.

She didn't flinch. She smiled slightly. "But that's okay with me."

I tried to relax. The topic was making me tense, almost hostile. Gretchen had done nothing to occasion it; I had to remind myself of that.

"The ironic thing is," she continued, "if I'd known you were back in town—and free from Steve Sayres—I'd have called you right away." Her thin, lavendered lips pursed. "Corporate lawyers wouldn't be right for us, even if they wanted a case like this. And a lot of lawyers, especially First Amendment types, have agendas. Some would be nervous about the anti-sex feminist opposition, some would want to turn this into an us-versus-them political thing."

"Turn what?"

"Margaret's not the only one. The ironic, truly crazy thing is, her partner—did she tell you about Arabella?"

"She didn't refer to anyone as her partner."

"Non-monogamous, perhaps, but still . . . Anyway, Mike's been contacted by Arabella's attorney. Apparently she's thinking about suing." She squinted at her window, looking a little confused.

"On the same grounds?"

"Arabella's not recognizable on the videos either, but that's because she's a porn star. She'd have eclipsed the point of the films, which is to make people think about their sexuality in a different way." Gretchen leaned toward me. "It's the fact of having one's image changed. We're finding it disturbs people. We're not sure what Arabella's particular problem is. She may think the tapes would have enhanced her career if they hadn't been reimaged. Her attorney requested unretouched masters."

I knew with uncomplicated immediacy that I liked the case, that I wanted it. The changing of video images: it was new ground. The perfect launch for my office.

"Are you authorized to speak for—what should I call him?"

Her smile widened; fondly, I thought. "Mike, Mike Hover. Or Brother. It won't matter to him. But yes. He authorized me to retain a lawyer for him. I can't represent him, since I'm in one of the videos. The same holds true for some of the other lawyers in our group."

"I would need to have it in writing from Margaret that she chooses not to proceed. I also learned some things from her that were privileged. I'd need to have it in writing that to the extent those facts are available to me from other sources, I can use them in spite of the lawyer-client privilege." I still wasn't covering my ass well enough. It would be a close call if Margaret raised a stink later. I should contact someone at the State Bar; run this by them. If the guru's retainer proved sufficient, maybe I'd contract-in a clerk to do that.

"All right. Why don't you talk to Margaret, then get back to me? Assuming you get her okay, would the case interest you?"

"Yes."

"Then I have no problem with discussing it with you this morning."

That was ballsy. I might still end up representing Margaret in a suit against the guru. I'd be able to use anything she told me, use it against him.

But Gretchen was a lawyer; she knew that. She was obviously confident Margaret would oblige. Maybe that implied duress. It bothered me.

On the other hand, it would do Margaret no harm for me to learn what I could. I'd have to be careful; that's all. I was on shaky ethical ground.

"If you'd like to tell me what Mike Hover has in mind, that's up to you. You know I don't have the documents I need from Margaret yet."

"I know. I just feel that you'd be best for this. I know you from law school, I know who you are. And I know the quality of your work by reputation. You're not beholden to a bunch of stuffy partners, and you've got very little else on your plate right now. You're perfect." She sat back. "You're a gift."

I had to smile. I'd never been called that before.

"How did you get involved with the group?" I wanted this to work. In spite of the videos, in spite of my anti-master bias, I wanted this case. It was novel; it would be interesting. It would very likely get some press, make people aware of my new office, people other than bankers. It could affect the direction of my practice.

She examined her manicured nails. "I think initially it grew out of what this profession does to you. At least, it coincided with my making partner." She glanced at me, the hint of an ironic smile on her lips. "I don't know how it's been for you; you've had some truly spectacular cases. But I think if you took a poll, you'd find a lot of lawyers ready to bail out."

It disturbed me to hear her echo Margaret; it sounded almost concerted. But then, both women had been in the same situation for roughly the same number of years. Long enough to burn out, to want more.

She smoothed her skirt. "I'm a partner now. It has the obvious rewards. It also has some major liabilities. I try to make the best of it. Occasionally a case engages my interest, but . . . about the time I made partner, I realized I didn't have anything else going for me. I'd gotten what I wanted, but I'd pretty much given up my free time, everything I used to be interested in that required a time commitment. Including an interior life." She anchored her strawberry hair behind a pearled ear on the unrazored side. "Anyway, I tried some of the usual stuff—you should see my antiques. And then I heard Mike speak."

My own mid-career crisis, running off for several months to the wilds of the Pacific Northwest, suddenly seemed sensible and tame. At least I'd gotten the bile out of my system, though it had cost me my savings. At least I wasn't forever immortalized in a porn flick.

"How did you hear about him?"

"I had an insurance defense case where one of the claimants became a devotee. We were tracking her, trying to show that her range of movement was greater than she claimed. And we found she was suddenly taking physics and optics and computer classes, going to salons, I guess you'd call them—the old-fashioned French kind—at Mike's house. She apprenticed at a hologram gallery. Her whole style of life changed. Intellectually, I mean—not in any way pertinent to the insurance claim. But I became curious, it was such a shift in focus."

"Did you join Brother Mike at that point?"

"No. I took mental note. Whenever I heard anything about him, I followed up on it. About six months later, I heard him speak—he was still living down here. I introduced myself, and we started having the most magnificent conversations. You know what it's like being around lawyers all the time—gourmet cooking and tame little kayak trips and effete chat. Mike brought me back into the world, with all-night rap sessions, very smart people discussing philosophy and science. Real stuff. Exactly what I was hungry for."

The same story Margaret had told. And why not? I was hungry for those things, too. I'd felt it when Dan Crosetti came to me with principles that had cost him every material and most physical comforts.

I looked around Gretchen Miller's office, and wondered how her new philosophy had changed her life. Her work life had remained the same, certainly. And the only glimpse I'd had of her off-hours life had chilled me.

"This was almost two years ago," she continued. "It seems much, much longer because it changed my whole orientation."

"If it's a matter of exposing yourself to new ideas, why not just do that? Why do you need a—well, what do you call him? Your guru? Your master?"

"Teacher," she answered matter-of-factly. "Or spiritual brother—that's why we call him Brother. He didn't choose that title, his followers pretty much foisted it on him. He wanted us to call him Mike, but to most people it didn't feel right. We know him to be a more philosophically evolved person than we are—and certainly a much more brilliant and scientifically gifted person. We'd have called him Father, if he'd have put up with it."

"Tell me more about the philosophy, about the group."

"We basically believe in a holographic universe. That's a rather popular theory right now—just step one in our thinking. Have you heard of it?"

"No."

"Well, let's see. How do I explain it? Did you know that holograms are projected by shining a laser through a piece of holographic film?"

"Go on."

"Well, if you take a piece of film that has, say, a dog on it, and you cut the film in half, each half will project the entire image of the dog."

"Hm." I found that mildly interesting. Certainly not profound.

"It doesn't matter how small you cut the pieces, each piece has the whole image encoded in it. That's the result—somehow—of interference patterns when a single beam of light is split and manipulated to hit the photographed object from different angles. Anyway, the point is, if the theory is correct—and it's the only theory that takes quantum physics into account—then the entire universe, including us, is like the holographic film. Everything everywhere has the complete image encoded into it."

"Sounds like high-tech Buddhism."

"In a way. It's really about tapping into more—getting glimmers of the all. You can put an infinite number of images on one piece of holographic film. The one projected depends on the angle of the laser. Reality is like that. We're finding tools to project some of the other things encoded on the film. Does that make sense?"

"It's as much detail as I need." I watched her, utterly calm and cool in her braid-trimmed suit. Even her philosophy seemed compatible with a lawyer's willingness to marshal facts, do research, construct a theory. No Eastern religion would satisfy that desire to proceed scientifically.

"Any fool can see our culture's ways of thinking about reality don't account even for our own experiences. We all experience telepathy, luck, synchronicities, memories of events we haven't seen, déjà vu, and on and on." She shrugged. "It's interesting to wonder about the mechanics of it all. I'd never even heard of quantum physics before I met Mike."

"How does the sexuality stuff fit in?"

"There are certain things about us as a species that seem universal. The seven deadly sins, that kind of thing. Our emotional behavior patterns, which he calls 'energies.' We observe them, play them out, see where they take us. We're trying to figure out what they tell us about the image on the film. About reality in a broader sense."

"I've seen the videos on the, um, sexual energies. So I've heard a bit of the theory."

"We also have workshops and salons on a huge range of topics—from Maya to Macintoshes. I've never met anyone as knowledge-able or as unhampered and intuitive in his thinking as Mike."

"What made you decide to participate in the sexual sessions? If you don't mind my asking."

She looked out the window. "That's one of my issues."

"What do you mean?"

Her color deepened. I felt myself flush in response. She wasn't my client. And this was personal stuff.

"Well, Laura, here's my agenda. I would like to try to keep this from coming out about me. But I used to hook in college. It's how I made my tuition."

It was all I could do not to blurt out my astonishment. More than that, my inability to believe it.

A sheltered girl from a small town, that's what I still was, I guess. Or maybe a privileged creature with a prissy belief that only "they" were prostitutes—tawdry blue-collar women without the brains to keep from being used. A different class.

"I had mixed feelings about the making and especially the dis-tributing of the tapes," she said, meeting my eye now. "Because whatever you think about it on a moral level, prostitution's a shit job—no protection for the worker whatsoever. And all the hookers I knew who were doing movies, well, they were basically hooking on film. Some of them got very bad deals. Once they were in the studio, there was no one looking out for them. And it's very diffi-cult work. If you don't keep yourself psyched, you can't do it. And there's that voice in you all the time telling you you're just letting yourself be abused." She paused, sighing. "But then, I used to feel that way working in department stores, too: pushed around by a bunch of officious, powder-cheeked women who wanted me to just *love* being part of the Nordstrom's family." Her fists clenched. "I'm not always the happiest little camper. But anyway, the point is that I have a lot of sexual issues. It's what Mike calls my defining field. It's what I needed to work on."

"You talk about hookers in porn films feeling used. You don't feel that way about the video you made?" I was having trouble maintaining eye contact. I kept remembering the expression on her face as the older man thrust into her.

"No. Because I wasn't pretending to like it. I was reacting honestly. And in public. To me"—her face looked damp now, with a waxy whiteness around the eyes and down her fine-boned nose— "it was a kind of catharsis, I guess. A way of taking back the pretending. Does that make sense?"

She watched me so earnestly that I wished I could say yes.

"WELL, NOW," Sandy finally said. He'd been standing over my restaurant table looking down at me for maybe a minute.
"You look fine."

I let him seat himself across from me. If I rose, we'd have to em-
brace. I didn't know how either of us felt about that. I said, "I'm
glad to see you."

He nodded, glancing away.

A waiter joined us and we ordered our usual drinks, Stoli iced for
me and Anchor Steam for him.

"Did you get a chance to see any of the videos?" I'd left him a
telephone message last night listing the titles.

"Couple of 'em, yeah. I called around; they're available a lot of
places." He raised his brows, causing fine, sand-colored hair to fan
over his forehead. His eyes were bluer than I remembered, his face
just as lean and lined.

"I'm glad you saw them. But it looks like I'm switching sides. The
person who was going to be my client changed her mind. Assuming she has no problems with it, I might go to work for the guru
himself. He wants to retain me."

"How'd he hear about you?" His posture was a little stiff; his tone
cool.

"A woman I knew in law school is one of the guru's people. Gretchen Miller. She works for Millet, Wray and Weissel. She's also in the videos."

The hint of a grin. "And people think lawyers are stuffy."

"My ex-client, Margaret, talked to her last night. When Gretchen found out Margaret wasn't going to use me, she called me."

"Isn't that a little . . . incestuous?"

"I'm not sure it's going to work. I'll need something in writing from Margaret. And I need to know there wasn't any duress involved."

"You mean like they tell her she's going to hell if she sues them?"

"Basically. But I don't think that's it. Margaret recognized herself on the video, but I didn't. And I was watching for her."

A quick frown told me he didn't understand.

"Do you know what reimaging is, Sandy?"

"Reimaging? Don't think so."

"The guru changes people's facial expressions—and I don't know what else—using computer animation techniques. So devotees who don't want to be recognized won't be."

"Slick." Sandy was unusually impassive.

"Apparently he gets very elaborate in the non-distributed videos; he puts in auras and things."

Sandy accepted his beer from the waiter. I flicked the lime wedge off my glass rim.

"In terms of legal ramifications, it's new stuff, Sandy. Interesting, maybe ground-breaking. Remember the tribe that wouldn't let anthropologists photograph them? They believed photographs stole their souls. You know people are going to have problems with being reimaged. Someone's bound to sue over it pretty soon." I didn't add, If I'm lucky.

"Ain't that the way of the world. You changed sides fast enough."

I took a sip of my Stoli. Spent a moment examining the restaurant's artwork, urban updates of Matisse. I didn't want to be goaded.

His tone softened. "I haven't been to this place in almost a year." Since you went away, he didn't need to add.

The place was purely my taste. Bright colors and scoured wood, California cuisine, killer salads. Sandy would have gone for heavy Italian food someplace dark and airless.

"It could turn into a hell of a case, Sandy. I'm lucky to get this client." If it bothers you that I feel that way, tell me now. If you can't work with me, tell me now.

"Yuh," he said. "I can see it's up your alley. What's the plan?"

"The first thing is, get a retainer from him. Then work out a fee arrangement with you." I watched him butter a triangle of flatbread. "If you're amenable."

His brows sank and he toyed with his butter knife. "My gut reaction? It's going to be hard to work something out. Sayres has me on that mega-retainer, so I don't mind putting in a lot of time for him. But by the hour, you could definitely find a more cost-effective fellow."

"I'll get us separate billing, if you're more comfortable with that. The guru's organization can pay you directly."

He shrugged, chewing the bread. "Not that I think you can't afford me. Just that you could get the same service at a better price."

So we were business associates now. Just friendly enough for him to try to save me a buck.

"What's your point, Sandy?"

"That you're not on Sayres's dime anymore."

"Yeah, and I'm not on his chain, either." I could feel my face grow hot.

"I heard you threw Sayres out yesterday." A grin stretched Sandy's face. I felt a rush of feeling for him, seeing it.

"I guess I did. He was posturing for his clients, acting like my kind uncle. And the whole time he was telling me he wouldn't have given me a reference if I'd asked for one."

"No shit?" He looked genuinely surprised.

"He basically accused me of killing Doron."

Sandy shook his head. "You must have got that part wrong. He knows better than that."

I sat back while the waiter placed my salad in front of me. Warm Brie over baby greens and walnuts. No use looking for anything like it in the small town I'd left behind.

I watched Sandy scowl at his plate. He didn't get it, never had: Steve Sayres hated me. Doron was Daddy; and Daddy always liked me best. That's what it came down to, really.

"Did you think I was being hysterical? I don't usually throw people out of my office." I stabbed my arugula.

"I know you've got no use for Steve."

"There's a reason for that." Sayres—men in general—enjoyed a presumption of rational behavior. Every time I got martial, people agreed I was a bitch. "I don't want to spoil my lunch talking about Sayres."

I watched him slice into a thick calzone, certainly the heaviest thing on the menu.

He said, "So what do you know about this guru?"

"Almost nothing. I know his name: Michael Hover, aka Brother. What do you know about him?"

"Well, I can't say too much without getting into who my client was and the nuts and bolts of that case. But I can tell you he's got his own little bitty island up in the San Juan chain off Washington State. A good percentage of his followers are lawyers and other professionals. They throw cash at him like you wouldn't believe. He's got so much gift income, he pays almost no taxes."

I listened with interest. "It sounds like he's found the right peg for the right hole. From what I've heard lately, lawyers are dying to get 'real.'"

He nodded. "Lawyers I work for are feeling pretty damn sorry for themselves. More than I ever noticed in the past."

Sandy had been doing investigations for law firms since 1968, when he'd quit the Los Angeles police force. Maybe the general dissatisfaction involved more than length of time in practice. Maybe the nature of lawyering had changed. Maybe the profession had grown rapacious in the demands it made on its practitioners.

"So he's got a lot of lawyers in his pocket?"

"And his hands in a lot of lawyers' pockets, yeah. He's into gadgets. He's not into politics. He doesn't have his people out door-to-door like Jim Jones did."

"Lawyers wouldn't go door-to-door." I couldn't imagine Margaret or Gretchen soliciting support. "It's a class thing. Haute versus petit bourgeois."

"Could be. It keeps his following small; he's got no one recruiting. But he does a lot of informal-meeting kind of stuff—people sitting around talking, or at least him talking at people. And sixties throwback stuff—encounter groups, sex groups, all that. That's about all I know about him. That isn't specific to my other case."

"Interesting." I watched him eat the calzone. He looked a little grumpy. I remembered him telling me once that he liked his pizza right-side out—when he could get it without fenneled duck sausage and artichoke hearts.

"I'm going to a rally at The Back Door tonight. One of the dancers used to be a big fish in Brother's pond. Now she's contacted a lawyer; she's asking for masters of his videos. I thought I'd check her out." I blissed out on my salad.

"Alone?"

"Well, it's a rally. Some kind of anti-censorship thing. But I thought I'd stick around for the show afterward. I want to see this person perform. It's not clear yet what her complaint is. It may be the reimaging; she's a porn star, so presumably she'd want to be recognized. The rally gets me down there, so I might as well see what she does."

With a sigh, Sandy put his fork down. "I've been in there on other cases, Laura. You can't go alone. Not if you stay for the regular show."

"Why not?"

"You're going to be the only woman in there wearing clothes."

"I realize that."

"Well, I guess you're one lawyer can't complain her job's full of the same-old same old." He rubbed his thumb over his chin as if checking for stubble. "I could go with you."

"I can't pay for your time unless the guru becomes a client. That might happen by the end of the workday—I'll let you know. But regardless, I can't pay you till I get the retainer."

"I'll go on spec." He shrugged. "Worse ways to spend an evening, I guess. Got to be better than *Idomeneo*."

He hadn't liked the opera I'd dragged him to a few years ago.

I reached my hand across the table. "Missed you, Sandy."

And I wish I'd listened to you: wish I'd kept my relationship with Hal familial. We'd have been friends now, Hal and me. Instead, he was gone and I didn't know if I'd see him again. The bastard, without even saying good-bye.

"Missed you, too, Laura." He gave my hand a quick squeeze. "But I guess you know that." He turned his attention to his calzone.

We ate in silence for a while.

9

SANDY RANG MY bell at about six-thirty. Traffic had been heavy and I'd only been home twenty minutes, time for a fast shower and a change into unwrinkled clothes.

He looked surprised when I opened the door. My shirt was flannel, my jeans faded, my shoes comfortable. I'd developed a preference for the wash-and-wear comfort of rainy-climate clothes.

"New place," he said.

I waved him in. The apartment was larger than my last. But the neighborhood, a neglected enclave between the avant-garde bustle of Castro Street and the middle-class stolidity around Mission Dolores, brought the rent down. And the place needed paint, needed its floors stripped, needed new curtains. My furniture, battered as it had become, dressed it up.

Sandy looked around. "Thought you'd sublet your place. Thought you'd move back there."

It didn't feel right, baring my financial soul. The fault was mine; I hadn't made my limits clear. What I hadn't spent on Hal's medical bills and on what I'd hoped would be a healing hermitage, I'd spent on scuba gear and dive trips with Ted McGuin. Sure, I felt a little bitter now. They'd been expensive boyfriends, and it wasn't clear to me what I'd gotten back.

"This place cheaper?" He eyed me coolly as he spoke.

"Quite a bit."

"Pricey location, your old place." He continued watching me. "But you had your golden parachute."

I looked up at him, at his crinkled cowboy face and seen-a-lot blue eyes. We'd been able to work well together, to do everything well together, because we'd always been direct. He knew what had depleted my White, Sayres severance package. He was asking me to put it out where we could talk about it.

If I didn't, our relationship remained professional.

But I didn't need to hear his "I told you so." I'd heard it in my head often enough.

I changed the subject. "It's all set with the guru. I got it in writing from yesterday's client that the switch is okay with her. I'm flying to the guru's island in the morning to meet with him and get our retainer."

He nodded.

"I'm not exactly hot to go to The Back Door. But I want to see this dancer. I want to see what she does. It might become an issue if she decides to sue."

Sandy knew I always scoped out parties' places of employment and other potentially relevant locations; there was no need to explain. The justification was for my benefit. I'd never been to a sex club.

"My car or yours?" He fumbled for keys in his anorak pocket.

"Yours." I didn't relish parking my Mercedes 380SL in the Tenderloin.

He held the front door open for me. I glanced up at him on my way out. His face was grim. Since he knew what to expect, I took it as a bad sign.

10

THE CLUB was a big stucco box painted black with gold stars and silver moons. The marquee announced show rooms and times—Naughty Showers in the San Francisco Room; Space Girls in the Ultimate Room; Crime and Punishment in the Berlin Room— plus The Big Show, Private Rooms, Lap Dancers, and Continuous XXX Videos. "Tonight from 6 to 8," a hand-lettered sign announced, "a Benefit for SF-FASE (San Franciscans for First Amendment Sexual Expression): Keep Fun Legal."

I'd walked and driven past this club dozens of times on my way to the State Court and the Federal Building. I'd averted my eyes from glossy photos of arched-back, long-haired women in posed pouts. I'd averted my eyes from the smirking men out front.

It seemed surreal now to follow a cabload of Japanese tourists through the front doors.

Behind a counter, a sleepy-looking young man sold tickets for twenty-five dollars apiece. A sign propped in front of him announced explicit sex acts within and warned anyone offended by such acts not to enter.

The ticket seller told the Japanese men that the Main Room was closed until eight o'clock for a benefit. They all nodded in nervous nonunderstanding and paid their money.

Then he looked at me. "You're here for the benefit. Sliding scale, fifteen to fifty dollars. Pay at the Main Room."

I pulled out two twenties and a ten and handed them to him. "We're staying for the other shows, as well."

He took the money, averting his eyes. I was apparently buying a lack of scrutiny.

"Enjoy the shows." He brandished a rubber stamp.

Following Sandy's example, I let him touch it to the back of my hand. In riotous script, the ink read "Sex-Positive."

He kept his eyes lowered. "Main Room is straight down the hall."

Men milling around the lobby saw me and quickly looked away. Each stood apart from the others, reading show-time signs or checking his wallet. They didn't glance at one another.

Sandy put his arm around me as we walked past the ticket counter. I turned and asked the ticket seller, "When and where can we see Arabella de Janeiro?"

His already closed expression clamped tighter. "She may be part of the benefit."

I'd taken Margaret's word for it that Arabella would be here either during or after. I hoped she hadn't been mistaken.

We walked down a carpeted corridor, brightly lighted. To our left, thick velvet curtains hung beneath a sign that read "Films." I stopped, taking a breath.

At the end of the corridor, under a "Main Room" sign, a large group was assembled. I was relieved to see a fair number of women. As we drew closer, I noticed many had dressed for the occasion, in tight leather and rubber and metallic vinyl.

Some must have been part of the show. Their bodies were dramatically voluptuous, and their dresses flashed more than teasing glimpses of breasts and buttocks. They mingled with spike-haired groupies with multiple jeweled ears, lips, and noses. One autographed a nude poster of herself: "Make me wet," her loopy script requested.

Beside them were knots of stagy transvestites, a more common sight; and a fair number of just-off-work professionals in business suits. A few long-haired old men appeared to be, and perhaps even were, beat poets. Several couples looked like me and Sandy, like intelligent—and slightly uncomfortable—liberals. Others in the throng wore nothing but body paint.

We stopped at a card table laden with pamphlets and paid middle-scale admission. We threaded through the crowd and stood in the back of a room painted black like an avant-garde theater. The ceiling was tracked with lights that hit a polished wood stage lined with stripper poles. There were four rows of seats on three sides of the stage, so everyone had a close view of two women acrobatically dancing and licking each other's bodies.

I was struck by how beautiful they were. Their figures were utterly perfect. Maybe I'd assumed models in girlie magazines were airbrushed and retouched. These women weren't. They looked like anatomically correct Barbie dolls.

As they concluded their dance, a voice from a speaker boomed, "Oh, yeah, aren't they gorgeous? Aren't they hot? Now don't forget, even though this is a benefit, that doesn't mean you can't tip. Show these dancers how much it means to you to be sex-positive. Show these ladies how much you appreciate living in freedom. Freedom of expression means no repression and a lot of sex-pression. So come on, now, be generous with those tips."

People tossed dollars onto the stage, which the women gathered as they minced around, shaking their fannies and running their hands over their breasts.

As they disappeared behind the curtain, a redhead in skintight black took center stage. "Thank you again for coming here tonight and showing support. As you know, sex workers have finally begun to have a real voice in their own employment."

A loud whistle and shouts of "All right!" from the audience.

"We've begun to shape some traditionally male areas of entertainment like porn films into something that both straight women and lesbians can get very turned on by. So we're especially happy to see that right now, when we're just beginning to find our voices and take some control, we have your support. Because, as you probably gathered from the disruption earlier, as we become empowered to make some wonderful changes, there is that part of the anti-sex, anti-porn, so-called feminist movement that would shut us up and shut clubs like this one down. And I call that censorship. I call that a lack of understanding about what it means to be a sex worker."

To our right, a group of leather-clad women, too assorted in shape and age to be dancers, began whooping and waving fists.

"Yes, that's right," the woman on stage shouted. "Let's tell them you can be a sex-positive feminist, and a sex-positive lesbian, and a sex-positive business person or librarian or whatever you are! Because sex is good, and sex work is good work!"

"Right on! Right on!" The audience response was country-bar jolly in tone and accent, as if the women were playing a role and having a lot of fun with it.

A voice at my shoulder said, "Hi."

I turned to find the blond lawyer from Hyerdahl's office standing beside me, still in that day's purple suit. She was grinning.

"I love this stuff," Pat Frankel said, glancing curiously at Sandy. "Naked breasts and butts and loudmouth lesbians. My kind of joint."

The speaker announced that she'd be reading an essay from her new book *Women With Short Red Nails*.

The three of us were forced back against a wall by people streaming into and out of the small theater. Behind Pat Frankel, a leering middle-aged man tracked the breasts of passing women. Beside Sandy, a tall transvestite, arms folded over his chest, cast darting, almost fearful, glances around the room. Naked people streaked with body paint pushed past, reeking of sex.

The woman onstage began reading a piece about two lesbians masturbating in a car. I could feel Sandy fidget.

I turned to Frankel. "Have you ever been here before?"

"Are you kidding? I got so nervous just walking up to the place I thought I'd chicken out. But I'm glad I came. I always wondered what it was like inside, what kind of shows they have."

"Were you here for the disruption she mentioned?"

She leaned closer, so our conversation wouldn't disturb others. "An anti-porn group. They came in and tried to grab the mike. Tossed literature into the audience—porn-causes-rape kind of stuff." She shook her head. "Even Nixon and Reagan couldn't buy themselves commissions willing to find a connection between pornography and violence."

"What happened to the women?"

"Hustled out. My whiner was with them—I'm doomed to see her everywhere, I guess." She joined the people around us in applauding the essay we hadn't listened to. "The protesters get points for costumes, though. One woman wore a giant Styrofoam tray with plastic wrap, like supermarket meat. Another one had a sandwich board plastered with weird pics from S and M magazines. A couple had bondage masks and fake blood, stuff like that."

The stage was taken over by a transvestite trio in high drag singing a Jerry Lee Lewis–style rock song titled, "Give Me a Licking."

We didn't talk through it. The singing was good and the lyrics were funny.

When they finished, a woman wearing lots of makeup and a frontless dress took the stage. She reminded us where we could find petitions, which organizations we could join or support tonight, and whom we could contact to express our sex-positive attitudes.

Enlivened by the rock-and-roll piano of the last act, I considered picking up some of the literature. The club vibrated with giddy energy. It was an interesting mix: sex workers, gays and lesbians, intellectuals, people who could belong to any profession, some in business attire, some in jeans.

Why force this kind of place underground? Most of what sold in this country was merchandised based on sex. It had been commercialized into a capitalist religion, with icons of bikinied women on billboards and TV screens everywhere. Protesting against strip shows seemed as pointless as cutting off a pit bull's tail.

The woman on the stage continued, "Now, don't think we're going to send you out of here tonight all calmed down, because our last act tonight, well . . ." She paused, her eyes closed, while a rap tune pounded from the speakers. She retreated as a woman in skintight polka dot shorts began a gyrating dance around the stage, her glossy blond hair swirling.

For a few minutes, the blonde engaged in pure tease—a flash of genital, a flash of breasts, lots of seductive licking of her fingers and squeezing of her nipples. Then a quieter jazz tune played. She pulled the halter and shorts off and spent most of the next five minutes displaying her genitals at the edges of the stage. There wasn't much pretext of dancing, just a lot of spread-legged Vs and on-all-fours undulating. Occasionally she turned cartwheels or did round-offs. Mostly she was on the floor touching herself or hanging over the edge of the stage with her large, perfect breasts in men's faces.

I wished I knew what Arabella de Janeiro looked like. I might be watching her now without knowing it.

Pat Frankel commented, "It probably enhances the show if you're a lesbian." From her rapt look, I concluded that she was.

But even from my less-susceptible vantage, I had to admit the dancer's routine required exceptional muscle tone and control. If she'd done it clothed on a gym floor, it would have looked like an Olympics warm-up.

Watching her collect tips, I could hear Sandy's deep breathing beside me. I could feel myself, totally and immutably heterosexual, respond to her beauty and gymnastic energy.

I looked at the stamp on my hand. *Sex-Positive.*

I whispered to Pat, "But it must be a hard job. It must be atrocious if you're having an off day."

"That's the truth no matter what your job is," she countered. "Can you imagine working at McDonald's with some pimply asshole bossing you around? Or being a motel maid and having to deal with body fluids on the sheets? Or being a farm worker, with all the pesticides they use now?" She looked up at me. "But I hear what you're saying. I just don't get why people single this group out and want to make them do something else for a living."

Sandy tapped my arm. I turned to find him glancing pointedly at my companion.

"Oh, I'm sorry. Sandy, this is Pat Frankel."

She extended her hand for shaking. "Hi. I work across the hall from Laura."

"Sandy Arkelett," he said.

"It's nice you came to this." She smiled as if it were her party. "I was happy to see you walk in."

"Did we miss much?"

"A couple of strippers, a reading. The outraged anti-sexers were the highlight." Her smile broadened; she'd enjoyed the strife. She addressed Sandy. "Did you like the show?"

"I'm with Laura, I guess. I can see why these women trade on their physical perfection. But there's got to be days it's near impossible to keep this positive attitude up. That's got to take its toll. And what for?" He looked around. "Get a bunch of strangers off."

"That's jobs in general. Talked to any lawyers lately?"

The MC came back onstage, reminding us about the availability of petitions and literature, and inviting us to come back soon.

As the three of us filed out with the rest of the group, I eavesdropped on conversations: a dancer introducing leather-clad lesbians to her "trainer," a dowdy older woman embracing a stripper and introducing her to another woman as "my wife, the porn star," a couple of bleach-haired, earnest men discussing an assembly bill, a woman in skintight stretch lace and four-inch heels telling a long-haired senior that she knew Ken Kesey, too. Several men and women complimented the performers with almost sycophantic effusiveness. I wondered if that was a function of the exaggerated respect liberals feel for "real" workers, or if it was sexual in nature, if these people had been turned on, and were, in essence, flirting.

We walked out with Pat Frankel, knowing our hand stamps would get us back in.

"You guys had dinner?" Her cheeks were flushed; she looked amped.

"We've got an engagement," I told her. "Can we take a rain check?"

I felt Sandy's surprise. We really weren't a "we," I guess.

"Of course." She took a step, waiting for us to walk with her. When we didn't, she moved on, saying, "Well, good to see you. Glad to meet you." With an impish smile, she added, "Talk to you tomorrow, Laura."

Sandy and I watched her leave. We stood out front a few more minutes until the rest of the benefit crowd dispersed. Maybe we were avoiding being conspicuous. Maybe we were embarrassed about going back in.

But seeing Arabella, checking out her workplace, was the point of this excursion. It might be my last chance to get a sense of her without her lawyer present, my only chance to learn about her work.

I would ask her no questions, of course. I would say nothing at all. I'd give her lawyer no excuse to make a fuss later. But I'd take careful mental note of what I saw.

11

THE TICKET SELLER seemed surprised to see me again. He muttered something about the benefit being over. "I know that," I said, showing him my hand.

I felt much more flagrant now. Men in the lobby stared at me, then turned away.

"Come on." I tugged Sandy's sleeve. If we didn't move quickly, I'd lose my nerve. The ticket seller's reaction told me I'd discover something different from what I'd seen at the benefit.

As we walked down the bright corridor, I found myself clinging to Sandy's arm. I was grateful he'd joined me. I'd have hated being alone here.

We passed an open door marked "Private Room; Separate Admission." Inside, two nude women sat on a large, low four-poster bed with a scatter of dildos, vibrators, and even, I noticed, a clear plastic speculum. On the other side of the room was a chair. Separating it from the bed was a filament strip I took to be an electronic barricade. One of the women called out, "We'll get real nasty for you. Buy a ticket and come on in."

I glanced at Sandy. His eyes drank in details of their anatomies, especially when one lay back and spread her legs, arching her back.

"Is Arabella in here?" Sandy asked.

The woman sat up with a sigh. "Well, she—"

The other woman preempted her. "You'll have to check back. We could take care of you now. Get real nasty." She held up the speculum. "Show you what it looks like deeeep inside."

Her look of phony ecstasy, worn like a mask, worn like the servile helpfulness of a store clerk or the elegant bonhomie of a maître d', seemed to put her miles away from us.

"Will Arabella be here later?"

"Check back," she repeated.

It was unsettling to get no confirmation that Arabella was working. I hoped Margaret had been right.

We headed down some steps into a room labeled "The San Francisco Room." It looked like a small nightclub with murals of people having sex in every conceivable position. Onstage, women licked each other under a lightly spraying shower. On padded tables in the center of the room, women lay on towels displaying their genitals to men who sat there. On other tables along a wall, women displayed themselves individually to lone men. Most were inserting fingers or dildos within inches of the men's faces. They were all very beautiful. They were all very young.

We heard one say, "Do you have a little inspiration for me?"

A man handed her what looked to be a ten-dollar bill.

"Do you have another one of those?" the woman asked.

He handed her another.

"What do you like? I have toys."

She pressed one into herself. "For a little more inspiration, I could put it deeper," she offered.

The women on the stage began lip-syncing to a song called "Sex-Positive." The lyrics basically said, We love it all the time in every way, we're the new kind of woman, we're sex-positive.

The patrons seemed pleased to observe their enthusiasm and pleasure—which I supposed was the point. I tried to imagine other workers radiating such passion for their toil. But it was hard to imagine miners singing about being "coal-positive."

"Surprised?" Sandy whispered.

I nodded, still gripping his arm. "If Arabella's not in the Main Room, let's go."

"There's plenty more—room with glass walls and suction-cup dildos, theater where you can see movies of scared-looking Asian ladies sucking—"

"I get the idea. I've seen enough to get a take on the place."

In the Main Room, three or four men occupied each row surrounding the stage, several free seats between them. On one man's lap was a gorgeous woman who looked about twenty, wearing a very sheer teddy. He kept his eyes on the stage as she braced her forearms on the seat in front of her and undulated in his lap. As I watched, she sat back, ran her hand over his cheek and whispered to him. He handed her a crisp bill, and she resumed rocking forward and back. I supposed this was the "lap dancing" advertised on the marquee.

Two other women wandered the aisles in bikinis or teddies and high heels, bending to whisper to the men, most of whom shook their heads. One man in the back, his hair matted and his skin pocked, nodded yes. The thought of lowering myself onto his lap nauseated me. The young woman didn't hesitate. She nuzzled against him, whispering in his ear.

As Sandy went to speak with the remaining dancer, the smell of sex—female wetness and semen—rose from the fabric of the seats in front of me. I hoped I hadn't touched anything; I'd have my clothes dry-cleaned, I'd scrub the hell out of my hair when I got home.

Onstage, a nude woman collected scant tips. Men could get closer views in the other rooms. They could see women do things to each other. They could go into a booth or into the Private Room and touch themselves. This was relatively tame stuff.

I watched the dancer, startled again by her physical perfection. I didn't have a bad figure—up until this evening I'd have said it was good. But these women were in a separate league. It was so much more dramatic than seeing photographs of starlets. I began to wonder if I'd judge myself differently when I got home and looked in the mirror. I wondered if the men in the audience viewed the women at home and at work differently.

Sandy returned as the loudspeaker boomed, "Isn't she hot? Isn't she wet? Isn't she stupendous? So head over to the Private Room now and see her in the flesh with another lovely and talented young lady. Go on over there and let them make you happy!"

Sandy shrugged. "Everybody's being cagey as hell about de Janeiro. Either she's not here, or she's put out word she doesn't want to be ID'd."

He turned me slightly, putting his body between me and various jostling men. I felt clenched, every muscle ready for a bolting exit. I'd never felt so out of place anywhere.

"You ready to go?" Sandy kept his hands on my arms.

I leaned against him. He inhaled sharply, wrapping his arms around me.

He was in the mood to have sex, I could feel it. And I could feel myself respond. Because it was the result of visual manipulation, my desire felt cheap and tawdry and somehow much more urgent. Maybe it's part of the drive to want what's lurid and outlaw and sleazy. I wondered how it would feel to make love with these images swirling in my brain. I wondered how it would feel to go with the cheapness of it.

It was heady, almost irresistible.

I hated getting sucked into rampant, panting I-don't-care-if-they-don't-mean-it desire. It swept over me and I hated it.

I took a backward step. "We'll ask the ticket seller one more time on our way out. If not, let's go."

Our final inquiry was fruitless.

On our way out the front door, someone handed me a button. Out on the street, I read it. It featured the ubiquitous slogan "Sex-Positive."

It sounded so clinical, like the results of an HIV or a pregnancy test. It sounded so Orwellian.

I stood there looking at it, remembering the wave of sybaritic desire that had washed over me in there. A hundred images flashed through my mind, *Penthouse* and *Hustler* come to life.

I looked up at Sandy and was suddenly worried that the images would never leave me, that sex would never be the relatively private and personal thing it had always been, that these women and this evening would crowd into my bed with me.

I guess Sandy read that in my face. "Same with police work," he said. "You never drive down the street that you don't see the people got knifed there and shot there, or who were lying there in pools of vomit. Once you actually see it, the world's different for you."

"I know that." A bit of an overstatement. "I just didn't think it would make me this uncomfortable."

I'd forgotten how consoling and caring his face could be. We'd clashed in my hometown. He'd hated Hal and he'd hated Ted and he'd lashed out at me. And I, chilled by four years of Hal's frost, had been determined to let Ted McGuin envelope me in his high-energy heat. I'd said some pretty harsh things to Sandy. He'd said some harsh things back. And looking back on it, we'd both been right.

"Look at it like TV, Laura. Or *Newsweek* magazine. It's a slicked-up bunch of bullshit images. You let go of them when it comes to your reality. You've got to."

"I feel like showering for a week."

Suddenly he laughed. He put his arm around me and gave me a quick squeeze. "That's it," he said, "that's me. You always think of me as such a straitlace, such a traditional-values fellow." He cocked his head. "Yeah, I know you do. Well, now you know why. The shit I saw as a cop you wouldn't believe. I couldn't even describe it and you wouldn't believe it. So that's why. You liberals always think it comes from being puritanical, from wanting to protect our innocence or some goddamn thing. But that isn't even close. A person wants to take a step back into something cleaner than what he's seen. Those old-fashioned values, they're your week-long shower, you know what I mean?"

My hand closed around the "Sex-Positive" button. "Traditional values just means you don't want this stuff in your face. You put some clothes on it and it's mainstream television and Miss America."

"At least it's not a nineteen-year-old girl spreading herself in public for money."

I rested my head against his chest. I felt as if I were coming down from a major drug. I felt depleted.

"And what the hell any of this has to do with religion and guru stuff, I don't even pretend to know," Sandy added. "You got yourself one very weird case here, you know that?"

"I've got myself money in the bank."

He chuckled. "Inspiration."

"That's right." I nodded. "For a little inspiration, I'll put it in deeper."

12

I'D TAKEN A long shower, trying not to notice my reflection in the bathroom mirror. I didn't look like the young women at The Back Door. No one I knew looked like them; only Barbie dolls, only TV stars. And yet it was my forty-year-old body that looked wrong to me tonight. Twenty years ago, with breast implants, I might have aspired to such perfection. Now I was merely trim, reasonably fit after months of hiking. But somewhere along the way, my skin had lost some of its creaminess, some of its glow. There were pockets of crepiness where once there had been elasticity. It had never bothered me before; I hadn't thought about it much. I'd been living in my head more than in my body, perhaps. In my career it was essential to wear nice clothes. If your body wasn't a good rack for the accepted styles, that was a problem. But what did strippers do when they reached forty? Did they stay "sex-positive" when it no longer served a business purpose?

I climbed into bed feeling dispirited and unattractive. I was just nodding off when the phone rang. I checked the clock: 2:02. I picked up, thinking it might be Sandy, just returned home.

"Laura. It's Margaret." Her voice seemed thin and brittle, about to crumble under some emotion. "I know it's late, but—. I'm going crazy. Gretchen doesn't answer. I didn't know who else to call."

"What's wrong? What happened?"

"She called me. Arabella."

I sat up, pulling the comforter around my shoulders. "Did she say something about the videos?" Why else would Margaret phone me?

"She was hit in the face and stomach." Margaret moaned.

It took me a minute to understand: this wasn't work-related. "She was beaten up, you mean?"

"Ambushed. In the parking lot tonight on her way in to work. She's got cracked ribs, black eyes, a split lip."

I shuddered in the cold room. "What time was this?" Did it happen while Sandy and I were inside? Earlier? We'd asked a number of people about her; had they known?

"Around eight. That's when she usually goes to work."

So she hadn't taken part in the SF-FASE benefit, as Margaret had assumed she would. But perhaps she'd crossed paths with some of the throng as they made their way to their cars.

"Did anyone see what happened? Do you know who hit her?"

"Two men. That's what she said. She's . . . she didn't want to go to the hospital, she wanted to take care of it herself, but it was too bad. She called me."

I envisioned the crowd at The Back Door. I supposed she hadn't wanted to stagger into the middle of it and ask for help.

"I tried to take care of her, but it was awful. I took her to the hospital." Her tone chilled suddenly. "She thought Brother Mike hired the men. I told her he couldn't have. He wouldn't do anything like that."

That got my full attention. "You know I represent Brother Mike now?" So don't tell me anything you don't want him to know.

"Yes. I thought you should know. I had to talk to someone. Oh, God, it's so awful, Laura. You should see." There was panic in her tone: harm had come to someone she loved. And she wasn't sure her guru hadn't caused it. Not after what he'd done with the videos.

"Are you all right, Margaret?" Obviously she wasn't; she hadn't waited till morning to phone.

"Ninety percent of the time, Arabella doesn't call me. Why now? Why did she call me now? To make me feel terrible?" The last words came out like cap-gun explosions. "She's hardly talked to me since Brother started doing videos. After two years together, suddenly she was too busy. We were together two years, did you know that? That's a long time. Especially for an exotic dancer. It's hard to stay with someone who has sex with other people all the time. But I hung in. We hung in. Two years."

And what? She only calls when things go wrong? She only calls to worry you?

Margaret began to cry, a high keening that was barely audible. "I hate love. It's so debilitating, so embarrassing. I work on it and work on it, but I just can't keep it small enough." She swallowed a sob. "It doesn't seem worth it. My mom killed herself when my dad left. I never understood, I was so angry; but now I do."

I didn't like the direction the conversation was taking. "Margaret." I hoped my tone was bracing, not unsympathetic. "I know this is painful for you. Are you still at the hospital?" I envisioned her outside the emergency room. Or in the lobby waiting for visiting hours.

"I came back to get my car. I'm calling from my car."

"You're on your way home? Will you be all right?"

"Not home, no. I need to walk." Her tone became increasingly hysterical.

"You need to rest, Margaret. It's late. Arabella's being cared for. Things will look better when you're not tired."

"My mother was a poet, did you know that? Graciella Lenin. Every once in a while, some college offers a class on her poetry. She wrote a poem right before she killed herself, about why she had to keep walking. She wrote it while she was walking; you can tell, it's so scribbled. 'I walk on shards of memory like mirrors of myself in pieces, and each step grinds my image finer and I walk myself into bright dust.'"

"Where exactly are you?"

"Parking lot. The Back Door."

Why there? Had she driven Arabella's car to the hospital, returning now for hers?

"You can't walk around that neighborhood this late, Margaret." I shivered under my comforter. My old apartment had been warmer.

" 'I walk myself into bright dust.' That's what I have to do. So the pieces won't cut me."

I wanted to crawl deeper into my bed. I didn't want to deal with this woman—a mere acquaintance—and her pain.

"My mother went to where my dad worked and she stood out front for a long time, and then she threw herself in front of a truck. It had mud flaps with silhouettes of naked women on it. Big old truck—I stared at it afterward, because it crushed my mother. They found the poem in her pocket. It was stained, but I let them publish it. Dad didn't want me to. But I saved it. And when I grew up, I let them publish it."

"Margaret!" I imagined her outside the theater waiting for a passing truck. Could she be that upset? "Please don't—"

"And now I totally understand it. About the memories being like shards of mirrors."

"Where exactly are you, Margaret? In the parking lot in back?" Sandy had parked across from the building's rear entrance.

" 'I walk on shards of memory like mirrors of myself in pieces, and each step grinds my image finer and I walk myself into bright dust.' "

"At the very least, why don't you drive home and maybe take a walk there?" My old neighborhood was relatively safe if she didn't get too close to the Presidio.

"I have to go now." A sob. "You stand up for yourself all the time, don't you? You tell people what you really feel."

I listened for background sounds, but heard none. "Margaret, are you okay to drive?"

"No. I won't drive. I'll walk. Walk myself into bright dust."

"No. Wait there for me. Wait in your car. If you want to walk, we'll go together to . . ." I tried to think of a place two women could walk safely in the middle of the night. "Will you wait there?"

"My mom believed love was a superior form of intelligence, pre-verbal and more powerful than intellect or sensory intelligence. It's in her poems, if you want to read them."

"Will you stay there and wait for me?" God, I didn't want to go out. I didn't want to be cold. I didn't want to be in the world. I didn't want to see anyone, much less someone going crazy. "Margaret?"

"Brother Mike talks about genuine love, where you transcend who you seem to be, and bond—I forget what part of the brain you bond in, but not the surface areas, not the intellect. Because obvi-ously, intellectually you wouldn't want to be with someone who sleeps with so many other people, would you? You'd want fidelity, wouldn't you?" Her voice was reedy, tiny.

"Will you wait there? I'd like to talk to you in person. Okay?"

"It's not easy to feel compared. You know, your partner sleeps with all these perfect-looking women. And they're so young; you have to give up food and get a face-lift to look even half as good. Sure, you tell yourself it's totally separate for them, their emotional life and love and all that, and sex. The others are just fuck buddies. It has nothing to do with you. Or with love."

"Margaret?" I was despairing of an answer. "Will you wait there, please? So I don't go out in the middle of the night for nothing?"

"Even if you tell yourself, okay, I won't worry unless she actually falls in love, well . . . We all love Brother Mike—but she had to make it personal."

"Or, Margaret?" I was cold and tired, feeling selfish. "You wouldn't want to take a taxi to my house? I'll call it for you."

"The sad thing is, Dad's relationship with the other woman didn't last. He should have known it wouldn't. It was all for nothing."

Not "My mother should have known; my mother should have waited."

She was experiencing both traumas, past and present. I knew she wouldn't put herself into a cab.

"I'm coming right now. Stay in your car. Lock your doors. I'll find you. Just hold off on walking—stay put."

I hung up. I almost lifted the receiver again to call Sandy. But I was no ingenue. I didn't need an escort.

If I didn't find Margaret after a short drive through the neighborhood, I'd consider calling him. I hated to think of her wandering that part of town. And two of us could cover more ground. In the meantime, he could get a little sleep.

I remembered how he looked, splayed across a bed with his lips parted and his hair down over his forehead. He looked like a rangy kid. He looked sweet. I wished he were here now.

13

IT WAS ALMOST two-thirty by the time I reached
The Back Door. I cruised slowly past the front, hoping I'd find Margaret parked there. There were a few people on the street: a young
women, cross-armed with cold in a minidress that revealed a mul-
titude of figure flaws; young men with tight jeans and oiled curls
throwing mock punches like kids in a playground; a homeless person clutching a bundle of freight; a man in a pea coat smoking a
cigarette.

I thought of my only night scuba dive. I'd been down with Ted
McGuin several times in the day. I'd grown used to thinking of the
ocean as a place of fish and seals and otters. But at night, with the
sea mammals up on rocks and fish motionlessly asleep in the kelp,
the world belonged to unfurling octopi, darting eels, gliding skates.

I circled the block, carefully checking the parked cars. None were
occupied. There were several cars in the parking lot across the street
from the building's back exit. Most were old and inelegant. One of
them, a dark, sleek Saab, might have been Margaret's. But like the
cars around it, it was vacant.

I circled the block again.

When I reached the front entrance, I noticed a man thumping
one of the doors under the marquee. I couldn't think what else to
do, so I pulled up and called to him: "Is there a problem?"

Perhaps Margaret had gone inside.

He turned toward me. He was a big man, square-jawed and weathered. "Fuck you," he said.

"I'm supposed to pick someone up here. Is anyone still inside? Do you know?"

He ambled toward my car. Damn Margaret. He looked as if he could rip my convertible top right off.

"Fucking doors are locked. Round back, too. And my lady ain't come out. Who you here for?" He squatted beside my window.

"A friend of one of the dancers. She called me for a ride. Have you seen anyone come out?"

"Not while I was in back. Maybe since I been in front." He looked chiseled from friable stone. As if he'd eased a hard life with alcohol and fistfights.

"You haven't seen a thin woman with a nineteen-forties hairstyle? Anywhere in the neighborhood?"

He shook his head. "Usually, everyone's out by now. What the hell's going on? Who's this friend?"

"Is there a pay phone around here?"

"Fuck you," he said, standing.

I watched him trot around the corner, waving away a woman in a vinyl miniskirt. She returned to slouching against a building.

I followed him in my car, parking in the side street near the back entrance. I climbed out, making sure the door was locked. The air smelled of beer and bay fog and cheap perfume.

If Margaret was inside, I wanted to know. I didn't want to waste time cruising the neighborhood. I wanted to go home and go to sleep.

I hurried around the corner. Light from a street lamp caught the building's silver moons and gold stars. I found the impatient boyfriend kicking what I took to be the wall. As I drew nearer, I saw the glint of a doorknob on black paint. The street was littered and still, facing the parking lot dotted with cars.

The man turned to me. "This is too fucking much." Then he bellowed, "Open the fuck up. Hey, in there!"

"Are you sure there are people inside? They might have left while you were in front."

He pressed his ear to the door. "You hear that? You hear someone crying?"

Again he kicked, a mulish, flat-footed blow beside the knob. The wood shuddered. He continued battering. The sound rang through the empty street. Finally, the door gave with a snap like a hewn tree.

When he hit it again, it yawned off its top hinge. He had to work at pushing it open.

I went in behind him.

We found ourselves in a corridor that, because it turned left, seemed to end ten feet in front of us. He disappeared around the corner. I was only five feet behind him, but I managed to stop before the turn.

I stopped because I heard a crack as loud as a cherry bomb. It echoed in the empty hall.

It shocked me to a sudden stop, shocked me because I'd heard that kind of sound before. I'd heard it boom through a ravine four years ago. I'd heard it, and found Sandy slumped against a tree, two bullets in his chest.

Now I heard a guttural, almost animal, grunt. I heard a thud. The man dropping? A finger of sulfurous smoke stung my nose and eyes.

I remained still, breath held, not wanting to understand what the sound and smell meant. In the black-with-stars corridor, I listened.

But I heard nothing else. Whoever had felled the man was either alone or didn't deem the action worthy of comment.

I began backing out. Where were the women who worked here? Had they attacked the man? Or had they been attacked? Rounded up in some room?

If so, there had to be more than one person involved. One to keep the women somewhere I couldn't hear them, and another to respond to the visitor in the corridor.

Or maybe the women were gone. Or gagged. Or dead.

Maybe including Margaret.

I was flat against the outside wall when I heard footsteps. The door, partly unhinged, was noisily scraped along the floor. I couldn't tell if it was being opened wider or pushed shut.

I waited there awhile, deciding what I'd do if the person came out. My menu was limited by inexperience.

But the person didn't emerge. I took a few cautious steps. The door was closed.

I began a panting trot back to my car, then stopped. I should stay where I could keep an eye on the door. At its odd angle, showing signs of having been kicked, it would attract attention. The first passing cop or curious passerby might investigate. Whoever was inside would realize that, would come out soon, would run away. There must be a phone nearby. I'd call 911 and return to watch—from a safe distance.

I surveyed the street: beyond the parking lot were closed Asian restaurants, sex-toy shops. I didn't see a pay phone, but if memory served, there was one a block up and half a block over, in front of a Chinese-language movie house.

I walked swiftly, relieved to be walking away, alarmed to be in this neighborhood in the wee hours of the morning. I lifted the strap of my handbag over my head so it traversed my torso.

I was hot, too pumped with adrenaline to feel the stipples of fog glazing my face and hands.

When I spotted the phone booth, I stopped. There were three men lingering near it, waving brown-bagged bottles and talking with much animation. If I approached, they'd think I was a hooker, treat me that way.

I felt a disconcerting sympathy for the prostitutes here. On-the-job harassment was probably more usual than not.

When the men finally walked on, I dashed to the booth. I hated touching the receiver, with its raised grime. I fished in my bag for a quarter, too flustered to recall I didn't need one for this particular number.

This would make the third time this year I'd dialed it.

I told the 911 dispatcher that someone might have been shot at The Back Door with a possibility of hostages held inside. She took the required information, her voice crisp and workaday. Though she asked repeatedly, a reflex of caution made me withhold my name.

With my adrenaline ratcheting down, I could feel the frost of dew on my face. I walked quickly toward The Back Door, goose-fleshed under my clothes.

Crossing the small parking lot, I glanced again into the Saab. On the passenger seat, spotlighted by a street lamp, were a stack of magazines and a paper bag. No court transcripts, no yellow legal pad, no briefcase. Nothing to tell me it was Margaret's car.

I looked across the parking lot at the rear exit to The Back Door. Even from across the street and halfway across the parking lot, I could see the door gaping.

I moved closer. The person who'd opened it had very likely left. Why else allow it to remain that way, an invitation for some vagrant to enter?

I stood there, wondering if I could let myself feel some relief. The miscreant was gone (I hoped). I'd already done my bit by calling 911.

Except that the man inside might need immediate help. I was totally unpracticed, but Ted McGuin, an emergency medical technician, had taught me basic first aid. I walked slowly closer. Maybe the police would arrive before I reached the building.

Maybe I'd think of a reason to remain outside. I might be wrong about the meaning of the open door. Perhaps the man hadn't been hurt. Perhaps he'd stumbled. Perhaps I'd heard and smelled a fire cracker. Perhaps he'd picked up his girlfriend and gone home. I had no actual knowledge anyone was in need of assistance.

In the few seconds it took me to reach the door, I changed my mind several times. I strained for the sound of an approaching siren.

I took a reluctant step inside. The malefactor was surely gone; surely that's what the open door meant.

My stomach knotted as I walked down the hall. When I reached the turn, I flattened against the wall and peeked around the corner.

On the floor was the man. Beyond him, more corridor, leading to places that were brightly lighted, but not in my line of sight.

I dropped to my knees beside him. His eyes were open wide, his lips parted, his skin pale; he looked like a wax figure. Stripped of surliness, he was handsome, younger than I'd imagined. The floor around him—but not, I noticed with relief, where I knelt—was pooled with blood. I didn't search for his wound. His bleeding had stopped, so had his breathing. He was dead, I was sure.

And my reason for being there had vanished.

I stood, more than ready to leave, listening for sirens.

The man had entered because his girlfriend hadn't come out yet. He'd said no one had come out. That might include Margaret. She might have come in here after speaking to me.

There might be people inside who needed the help I couldn't give this man.

But they weren't my responsibility. It might not be safe for me.

I backed toward the door. Where the hell were the police?

What was the average response time; hadn't I read it somewhere? Surely they'd respond quickly to a call that someone had been shot.

I remembered stories I'd heard, people waiting forty-five minutes or longer for help. People dying before anyone arrived.

I couldn't hear a sound. Maybe the theater was empty.

I took a few steps forward, being careful not to step in blood. I listened; heard nothing. I took a few more steps.

I made slow progress down the short length of hall. My own noises—shoes on linoleum, fast breathing, heart in my ears—were the only ones audible.

The corridor led to a locker room. It was littered with street clothes and duffel bags. I walked through it to a room resembling a walk-in closet. It was hung with gauzy feather-trimmed capes and spangled minidresses. High-heeled shoes, mostly black patent, formed untidy rows.

Beyond these changing rooms was an area of pulleys and ropes and black-painted floor strewn with lipsticked paper cups and open Coke cans. Chairs were draped with costumes. In front of me was an open black curtain. Five or six feet beyond it was a closed curtain.

I made myself walk toward it. I could stand here endlessly debating. Action would be quicker, maybe even less nerve-racking.

When I reached the second curtain, I took a steadying breath. I didn't want it shaking when I parted it.

I slipped my hand in at eye level. I moved it just enough to look through.

It was a slice of the Main Room, with its four rows of seats in front of the strippers' stage. The seat directly in my line of vision was occupied. I could make out a sliver of stretch lace: one of the dancers. Wearing some kind of mask?

I wanted to believe, at that moment, that things were normal; that the dancers were sitting there unwinding; that's why they hadn't come out. That the locked doors had been a silly misunderstanding.

But I parted the curtain farther and learned better.

There was more than one dancer in the audience. The ones in my view were taped to their chairs with silver cloth tape, rows and rows of it wound around the seat backs. But that part was okay; that could be viewed with only moderate horror.

Their faces were wrapped with duct tape, too. They were completely covered over. Where features should have been, there was only silver, gleaming dully. Silver like opaque veils or metal gauze, like tin masks: my brain tried to make it into something I could comprehend.

The swaddling was convex at the nose, slightly concave where their mouths should be. It flattened their hair, pushing it into disheveled eruptions on top.

Blank masks. As if their faces had been glazed away. Lusterless silver, like unfinished robots.

I couldn't seem to avert my eyes.

I stepped through the curtain. Later, it was this action, more than any other, with which I reproached myself. To step into a room of bound, possibly dead people when not all the room is within view—the stupidity of it stunned me, later. The stupidity of it crawled into my nightmares with me.

It was a thoughtless surge of action, an oh-my-God of forward movement.

As soon as I was onstage, I became vexed by regret and dread; I was no neophyte, to rush into dire situations. In that apex of reproachful terror, I forced myself to walk to the edge of the stage and look down.

All six seats in the front row were occupied. Six nearly naked women were trussed there. The middle two slumped against each other. The others' heads lolled forward or backward. Only one sat more or less upright. She'd managed to squirm low in her chair despite the bindings. Her head was braced against the seat back, silver mask tilted toward me. A clotted red trickle traced her throat and cleavage. Adhesive binding pulled away the scant cup of her bikini.

Immobilized in provocative lingerie and gleaming facelessness, the dancers might have been performance art: The Interchangeable Women.

Immobilized. I felt myself yank invisible bindings from my arms. My father had left me with my "Aunt" Diana one winter while he traveled to Italy to sell his ancestral home. She'd caught me trying to sneak out a window, and she'd bound me to a chair and railed at me half the night while I bruised and bloodied myself straining to lunge at her.

I couldn't bear to feel trapped, to feel helpless; had to stifle screaming rage at the mere thought. I didn't dare imagine how these women had felt.

I don't know how long I stared at them. Long enough for the stench to reach me. Mingled with the smell of sex and sweat and cigarettes were the contents of relaxed bladders and bowels.

Only then did I rouse myself to help them; to make the gesture, though I believed it was too late. Though I presumed they were dead; suffocated under airless layers of duct tape.

When I started toward the stage stair, I finally heard the sounds I'd been listening for: loud footsteps, male voices. And then a cessation of noise that told me the body in the corridor had been discovered.

The police. I'd asked 911 to send help to the rear entrance of The Back Door. The police had arrived.

Hadn't they? I stared at the shackled, featureless women and thought; What if it isn't the police? What if it's the people who did this? What if they've come back?

My flesh went painfully cold; I felt as if I'd been dunked in ice water. What if the people who did this found me here? What if they taped me, too?

I stumbled down the stage stairs, shaking, panicking, trying to be silent. I couldn't let that happen, couldn't take the chance.

I tripped toward the bound women. But I didn't stop to help them, I didn't try to pull the tape from their faces.

Whoever had arrived would be in here soon, maybe momentarily. If it was the police, they'd undo the binding. If it wasn't, then, oh God, I had to get out of here. I had to get out of here now.

I heard a sound behind me. I wheeled, cursing the hesitation that had cost me my choice. I expected to see someone—maybe the police, maybe the killers—pushing through the curtain.

But the noise came from some distance behind the curtain, perhaps from the changing room. Whoever had entered appeared to be moving cautiously. Surely that was a good sign? Surely it meant the police had found the dead man in the hall and were proceding cautiously until reinforcements came. I should stay here. I should wait.

But if I was wrong, I could end up like the dancers, squirming in agonized suffocation.

I knew the way out.

I tried not to look at the mostly naked, very still flesh in the front row. I sprinted out of the Main Room and into the front corridor.

It was eerily bright, utterly empty.

In the lobby, I sank to my hands and knees, letting the ticket counter shield me from view.

Was I being stupid? If it was the police in there, they'd question my flight. It could play havoc with my career, maybe get me arrested.

I heard commotion in the Main Room. The bodies had been discovered. Or, having found the back empty, the murderers were no longer attempting to be quiet.

Knowing what I risked—either way—I crossed the last few meters of lobby to the double glass doors.

There were no cops out front. I took that as a bad sign.

I pushed on the lock bar. The door didn't give.

I denied myself the luxury of panic. I scrutinized the door and saw a key in the lock.

I wiped the bar with my sleeve, pulled part of my sweater over my fingers, and turned the key. If it was the police who'd entered, it would mislead them, finding the door unlocked.

I didn't want to mislead the police. And I wanted to believe they were in the Main Room; that I was in no danger. I almost wavered.

But I could almost feel the ripping pinch of tape on my skin. And I knew from recent scuba lessons how it felt to struggle for air.

I pushed the door open. I slid out the narrowest-possible aperture and I bolted around the corner.

My car waited in a pocket of shadow. I pulled my keys from my handbag and got myself inside. I tried not to rush; rushing might make me fumble.

I backed out of the side street with my lights off, backed out quickly. Vaguely, in the periphery of my vision, I logged night people, possibly the ones who'd lingered here earlier.

Wouldn't they have scattered if they'd seen the police arrive?

They were likely selling sex or buying drugs or were a little crazy to be on the street so late. Wouldn't they have dispersed?

I put the car into drive, certain now that I was running from killers. I clicked on the lights and fled. I jerked a fast half block, then forced myself to slow down, to observe the speed limit and not call attention to myself. Not until I was sure I hadn't run from the police. Because if I had, reinforcements would arrive soon. And I didn't want to be stopped for reckless driving. I was too rattled to explain. All I wanted was to be away, far away from here.

I drove slowly for an interminable block before I finally heard sirens, lots of them.

My rearview mirror caught distant flashes of red and blue lights. The police.

My God, I'd fled a crime scene. How would I explain that?

I hit the accelerator, my stomach cramping. It was probably the police inside, then. They wouldn't have answered an initial 911 call in such force. These were backups responding to a call for officer assistance.

I should stop now. Go back. Tell them what I knew.

But Jesus, they'd make life hard for me. I'd run away; how would they interpret that?

They'd detain me all night, probably most of tomorrow. I'd be explaining this for days, begging them to believe I knew nothing, that I'd gotten a phone call and come to help an acquaintance.

I doubted I'd be arrested; they would find nothing linking me to these murders: no blown-back tissue or splotches of blood or old feuds. But they would make my life hell because that was how they did their jobs.

And it wouldn't be just the police. When Wallace Bean and Dan Crosetti died, I'd been trapped by reporters, mobbed every time I stepped out, everywhere I went.

I couldn't bear the thought. I'd grown used to my privacy; it was all I had left.

And the publicity would taint my new practice. It might sink under the weight of doubt and innuendo. Wouldn't Steve Sayres love that?

I pressed my foot to the gas pedal. The car shot forward. Reporters around me night and day, the burned coffee and sour sweat of police interrogation rooms.

I couldn't put myself through it. I'd rather run.

But oh, my God. How would I ever explain this if I got caught?

THE PLANE FLEW low over vast mirrors of water and snow-capped volcanoes. I burrowed into my seat. I closed my eyes, hoping to achieve the sleep that had eluded me last night. But that meant dealing with my conscience and my fears, and that was the same old torment.

Where was Margaret? I'd driven to her house this morning and pounded on her door, hoping to narrow the scope of the tragedy, to console myself with proof that only strangers had died. But either Margaret hadn't been home or she hadn't been willing to acknowledge my shrill petitions for entry.

Had she gone to The Back Door? Had she changed into sexy lingerie and ended up taped to a seat? Had she seen the murders? Had she—for reasons I couldn't grasp or for no reason but sudden madness—killed those women?

Or had she wandered the night away and then retreated to a deep but innocent sleep?

Maybe she'd never even been to The Back Door parking lot. Maybe she'd sent me there for reasons of her own.

Had she sent me there to find six dead women taped to chairs? Or six live women I could rescue?

I opened my eyes. Why pretend sleep was imminent?

I'd spent most of the night cataloging things that could go wrong:

The police could find my fingerprints somewhere my earlier visit wouldn't explain. Someone in the neighborhood had noticed my car and remembered the plates. Margaret might come forward and tell the police she'd phoned me (before leaving the vicinity?); she might tell the police I'd planned to go there.

I tugged at my seat belt. Even one band of restraint seemed insupportable after last night's display.

If the police learned I'd fled, the State Bar would discipline me. Steve Sayres had friends on the Board of Governors; it was a sure thing. I'd spent ten months learning how much I needed my career. I didn't want it pulled out from under me now. Especially not by Sayres.

My practice, so frail and new, would certainly collapse under the weight of the negative publicity. There were plenty of untarnished lawyers in San Francisco. I'd be frozen out.

I stared out the window. Washington was so green and vast, so unspoiled. Maybe I should have stayed up north, where people valued simplicity and natural majesty, where things didn't come down to whom you knew and how you played the game. If only Hal hadn't grown so quiet, so disturbed. I could have loved the underpopulated woods. Maybe I could have made something of a country practice.

I indulged a brief fantasy of closing down my new office and moving back.

This morning, with seven bodies on my mind and my conscience, I'd have been happy to walk away from the big city. But I was determined not to be forced out.

I had a day to think things over and chart my course. I'd been grateful for the plane ticket taking me to Brother Mike's island. A nice, early flight so I didn't have to cope with morning news reports and the inevitable call from Sandy.

Sandy. It wouldn't be easy, keeping this from him. But my alternative was to make him an accessory after the fact to my flight from a crime scene. I was a better friend than that.

Beside me, Mount Saint Helens rose and then stopped, its top a ragged spill of gray ash.

Once I arrived in Seattle, it would take another hour and a half to reach the ferry to San Juan Island. It would take an hour to reach that island, and a half-hour motorboat ride to Brother Mike's island. I could count on another four hours of solitude on planes and buses and boats. I wished I had twice as long.

I stared out the window at the flat volcanic lakes and saw silver tape masks. I saw myself being met at the airport by policemen, being booked and jailed. I practiced learning that Margaret was dead.

I curled up in my seat, again hoping to retreat into sleep.

Again, it was no use. I pulled the credit-card phone out of the seat back in front of me. I called Sandy.

"Where are you?" he demanded. "Have you heard?"

"I'm on a plane to Seattle. I'm going up to Michael Hover's place. I told you that yesterday." I tried to keep my tone normal, but I could hardly remember feeling normal. "Have I heard what?"

"I've got some very weird news for you, I'm afraid."

I'd wanted to go to him last night. I'd wanted to take a hot cup of tea from his hands and tell him what I'd seen. I'd wanted to lie in his arms and feel protected. I'd wanted him to say he understood why I'd fled.

I shrugged tension out of my shoulders. The plane was small, but still, there was no one within two rows of me. I had no excuse not to ask. "What's the news?"

"Six women work at The Back Door got killed there last night."

"Killed as in 'murdered'?" I didn't want to feign shock. I might have to confess later—to him, maybe even to the police. There was a limit to how duplicitous I could be without burning my bridges.

"Yuh. Cops are keeping it quiet exactly how they died—won't release the names till later, till they've contacted all the next of kin."

"Was de Janeiro one of them?" I recalled the line of silver masks. Thought about the women I'd seen dancing. I'd spent most of the night trying not to connect certain faces with certain teddies.

"That much I know. De Janeiro's in the hospital. She got jumped earlier that night."

"What do you mean, 'jumped'?" This question, at least, was sincere. Margaret had offered very little information.

"It looks like someone held her while someone else hit her—she got banged up, bruised. But no scrapes or dirt on her clothes, so it doesn't seem like she fell down or fought back or anything like that. Like I said, probably someone held her arms while someone else slugged her."

"Is she all right?"

"They're not saying much, but I gather they don't check in people who've been beaten unless they're watching for internal damage. She's not in Intensive Care, so they haven't found any yet, apparently."

"Did she ID anyone?"

"What I heard is she won't say anything except that it was dark and it was over fast. But she could be lying—someone hits you more than once, they're probably in your face long enough for you to see them."

The plane was beginning its descent. I could feel it in my ears.

"Laura? You still there?"

"What time did this happen? What time did she go to the hospital?"

"Happened around eight o'clock, apparently. Which is probably why the women we asked were acting so strange: she was supposed to be there, but she wasn't."

"Did she go to the hospital right away?"

"Nope. Your used-to-be client, Margaret Lenin, took her to the Emergency Room around eleven. They cleaned her up and x-rayed her and let her go around midnight. They told her to come back if she spit up blood or passed out. Which she did—come back, I mean. They checked her into the hospital around a quarter to two."

"Where was she the time in between?"

"Hell if I know."

"Was she well enough to t——" I caught myself before I said, "tape up her coworkers." The police hadn't released that information.

I took a deep breath.

"Well enough to what?" Sandy's tone was reserved, almost suspicious.

"Well enough to go kill her coworkers?"

"Assuming she had a reason to do that. More likely whoever beat her up went to the theater later and killed the women. But to answer your question, I don't know. She's got to be hurting if they admitted her to the hospital."

"Was Margaret with her when she went back?"

"I don't know. I talked to someone in Emergency. All I know about her being admitted is what's on her chart."

I knew the charts weren't available for casual perusal. I was impressed he'd managed to sneak a look.

"Find Margaret for me, Sandy." I didn't want to tell him about her two A.M. phone call. He'd know I'd followed up on it; he'd know I'd gone to fetch her.

"All right." His tone was aloof. "Any particular reason?"

"She might know how badly Arabella was hurt. The possibility of her being involved with the murders aside, it might affect what Arabella decides to do about her lawsuit."

"All right." His voice said, "If that's all you want to tell me." "You got the guru's number for me? I'll phone you there."

I fished Brother Mike's phone number from my briefcase and read it to him.

I stared out the window, knowing there was more I should ask. Trying to think how I'd discuss this if I had no more information than I should have.

Finally, Sandy helped me out. "De Janeiro getting beaten—it might have been a hired job. Might have been a mugging. It's not high priority with the police—her kind of work, that kind of neighborhood. Or it wasn't till this other thing happened."

"They think the two are related?"

"I'd say the operating assumption downtown is someone had it in for the women, all of them. They got de Janeiro on her way in to work—maybe got scared off by the crowd leaving the benefit. Then they went back and got even more violent." A slight pause. "Don't you want to know how they died?"

"You said the police weren't releasing the information."

"Doesn't mean I don't know. I've seen the coroner's pictures. It helps to have friends."

I sat in rigid endurance while he described the scene to me. I didn't comment.

"You okay?" he asked finally.

"Yes."

A sigh. "I talked to a couple of people work at the theater."

I had to give him credit: the police usually wrapped their witnesses up tight. "What did they say?"

"The guy who was selling tickets left around one—got a call his wife and kid were in an accident. Turned out they were fine, so obviously someone just wanted him out of there—guy doubles as a bouncer. The dancers told him to go ahead and leave—they didn't have any customers; I guess weeknight business can be pretty negligible. So he went tearing off. The women were going to lock up after him. One of them was going to wait around for the clean-up people."

"Were the women wearing street clothes when they found them?"

"No. Could be some customers came along who looked like real good tippers, and the ladies decided to let them in and do some more dancing. But I kinda doubt it. Could be one of the dancers made the call—that the women wanted him gone, but whatever they'd planned didn't work out right."

"That's an understatement."

"Probably whoever phoned the ticket guy was outside watching for him to leave. They probably went right in there with the duct tape. Didn't give the women a chance to lock up. Cops found the front door unlocked."

If I'd gone inside sooner, would it have made a difference? If I'd gone straight in to them and pulled the tape off their faces—"How long had they been dead when the police found them?"

"Not long." He stopped, seemed to listen hard to what I wasn't saying.

When had the last of them died? I wondered. Before I arrived at the theater? While I was at a phone booth calling for help? While I was edging along the corridor? When I decided to walk right by them and save myself?

"Laura?"

"You said something about a man, a dead man?"

"Did I?"

"Yes."

"Could be he kicked the back door in and someone greeted him in the hall with a gun. Or he might have been involved in killing the women. Cops don't know. They figure he died right away when the bullet hit him. Thirty-eight caliber. They haven't found the gun." When I didn't respond, he added, "I mentioned the women were taped facing the stage? I was thinking maybe someone wanted their attention."

I'd been so traumatized by being on the stage looking down at them that I hadn't considered what they'd been taped there to look up at.

"Who?"

"All I can offer is an uninformed guess. But they had a group of women there earlier in the day protesting. I heard your lawyer friend telling you about them. They might have gone there later to do a little coerced education. I tipped my cop buddy to find out who they were."

"They wouldn't kill seven people, Sandy." Would they? Or was I making assumptions based on feminists I'd known? Was I refusing to believe a philosophy to which I subscribed could be perverted to include violence?

"Who knows. Tell me more about Margaret Lenin."

The question chilled me. It was going to be difficult, keeping secrets from Sandy.

"She's the client dudded out on you, right? From the infamous videos?"

"Yes."

"But she's not your client anymore?"

"No."

"And you're not friends?"

"Acquaintances. She co-counseled me in on some of her cases when I worked for Doron. She's in-house for Graystone." Maybe I'd told him that at lunch yesterday. I couldn't remember.

"You'll be available later?" I could tell from his tone he knew something was up. "Laura? You'll be there when I call you?"

"We're about to land." I could see the Seattle-Tacoma airport now, a field of light-studded asphalt against a gray sky. "Bye, Sandy."

As soon as I hung up, I missed the comfort of his voice.

THE FIRST THING I said to Michael Hover was, "Before we get to the nitty-gritty, I'll need to have you review the retainer agreement. Please sign it if it's to your satisfaction."

He was not what I'd expected. I'd expected a smugly beatific man with a gift for glib aphorisms. Or an emaciated ascetic with a mad, brooding air. Or perhaps a spoiled man-boy surrounded by gadgets and fast cars.

The man sitting a few feet from me in an Adirondack chair wore dark slacks and a pin-striped short-sleeved shirt with a row of pens in one pocket. His hair was a thick, graying brown, and his face was surprisingly ordinary; someone's engineer uncle, that's what he looked like. He maintained almost constant eye contact and had one of the most soothing voices I'd ever heard, but otherwise there was nothing overtly guru-like about him.

He took the papers from me and began reading them.

I'd been ushered through his "quantum hostel," a whitewashed farmhouse with cushion-strewn wood floors. From the uneven stone patio in back, we had a view of the lush tiny island that took hours to reach. It was gorgeous, no denying it. Beyond a benign tangle of orchard, the sea shone a flat platinum. Mossy islands rose from a ribbon of mist.

I'd seen perhaps a dozen people so far, surrounded by books and notebooks in an extensive library, or plying mops or trimming mammoth hedges. I'd passed one room where a circle of devotees sat with heads bowed, saying nothing. Video cameras on tripods whirred at center circle. In the kitchen, two men and a woman communed with computers as vivid as televisions. At the sink, a man chopped chickens.

Brother Mike looked up from the papers. "I've heard what happened at The Back Door. Do you have any details?"

I felt my muscles knot. He'd found out quickly. "Only what's generally known, that six employees and a man were murdered." I wouldn't tell him anything I hadn't told Sandy, hadn't told the police; that protected us both from his conscience, if not mine.

"I know several of the women who work there—I met them through Arabella. It's been frustrating not knowing which of them."

"The police have probably released the names by now. At least some of them."

He paled. "Who should I call to get that information?"

"I'll take care of that for you, if you like. But it raises a point I need to discuss with you. Arabella de Janeiro was beaten last night outside The Back Door." I continued in a rush. "In my experience, it's unpredictable what a traumatic event like that will do to litigation plans. She may delay or drop the whole thing. She may blast ahead because she needs money to pay her hospital bills."

He sat heavily back. "Beaten? Badly?"

"Badly enough to require hospitalization, but with no lasting injury, I gather." My God, I'd asked Sandy so few questions about her—about someone who was planning to sue my client. Sandy must have found that astonishing.

"Who did it?" He watched my face as if reading an instrument panel.

"I don't know. I'm sorry; I'll get details soon. As soon as I get back."

He started to say something, then fixed an unfocused stare on the pines behind me. With a slight shake of the head, he resumed reading the agreement. Before he'd finished, he pulled a pen from his pocket and signed. His script was almost illegible, very back-hand. "I'll have Roy cut you a check before you go. I hope you'll stay the night."

"Thank you." I hated the thought of being surrounded by peo-ple all evening. After my antisocial winter, spring, and summer, I was having trouble adjusting even to small talk. It didn't outweigh my need for this retainer.

"Thank you. My flight leaves tomorrow." What I needed to learn about Brother Mike's videos might take more than a few hours. It hadn't made sense to book a same-day return flight. "I'd be happy to stay."

"Sometimes," he said, "I look around and wonder what the en-tity looks like to outsiders. If you can be honest with me, that would be a lot of fun."

"I'll have no trouble being honest," I assured him. "I'd be useless to you otherwise."

"Gretchen is impressed by your self-confidence."

"I notice you refer to this, um, place as an 'entity.'"

He rose. "Not just the place. The whole thing. Do you want to walk around, see the island?"

"Fine."

The house was ringed with evergreens and fresh-cut grass. The smell of sea and fir mingled. We walked through the yard and be-hind a stand of gnarled fruit trees. I was astonished to find what looked like an orchard of roses.

"I don't think I've ever seen such big bushes."

His murmur of assent made it clear he'd grown used to, even a little bored, with them. "The reason I call it an entity is it has a life of its own. Honestly, it does." He ran a hand over his thick hair. I noticed he walked with a slight stoop, paying no attention to his surroundings. "I've thought about this a lot and the best I can come up with is—well, I always liked to kick around ideas. I was very taken with Plato's *Republic* when I was a kid, with the depiction of Socrates as someone who didn't pretend to know the answers, and deflated anyone who thought he did. My starting point has always been: As soon as you fall in love with a method of analysis, it imprisons your thinking. It becomes jealous of competing analyses and locks you in like an angry lover. I used to spend hours trying to get my college friends to let go of their tight little perspectives and try out some other possibilities. I was surprised how many things they refused to even think about. They'd decided in advance, for instance, that there could be no such thing as telepathy or spirit or God—or lack of God—or no such phenomenon as a subatomic universe, or an implicate order of reality which differently manifests itself to different people. Or whatever. Things we can't possibly rule out—or prove."

"So you began assembling a group of"—what should I call them?—"followers back then?"

"You could say that. I always had ten or twelve other students in my dorm room, and I'd stay up all night arguing with them. All I really had to say was 'Let go of your way of looking at things because it keeps you from looking at things in other ways.' Not much of a message—although they argued furiously with me. After a while, around campus I'd hear people repeat things I'd said—and I didn't know a thing back then, truly. What I said would get changed a little bit. And then people would argue about that, and they'd come back to me with their arguments and I'd refute them—somehow the ideas became terribly pompous by the time they came back around. Solidified, as if I wanted people to believe particular things instead of just keeping their minds open. And it went on and on. Pretty soon it seemed like whoever was in my group—and that would change at least in part from year to year—we'd be arguing about different subjects. It was wonderful for me. I learned so much about how thinking gets constricted. That helped me take some huge intuitive leaps. That's certainly been true the last few years. I've been surrounded with intellectually nourishing companions."

I could understand his appeal, at least surfacely, for Gretchen

Miller and Margaret Lenin. He came on like a mentor, not a preacher. Unlike Jim Jones, he hadn't plugged into a fundamentalist Christian preaching style. He seemed more secular, more idea-oriented. But that was just a first impression. I hadn't heard any of his philosophy yet.

He stopped beside a bush of blown white roses with hips the size of apricots. He tapped one, watching its petals fall. "Most recently, the people around me have wanted to explore sexuality. A few years ago, I'd have said the group was political in its orientation; concerned with evolving an ethic that was de-rigidified and de-Americanized. They wanted to expand their thinking beyond what they'd learned in college core courses. But there was a shift, some people left, others came in. AIDS, I think, was a big factor. San Francisco's a very sexual town and it was a shock to it, closing the bathhouses, all this latex after years of freedom. The energy has to be expressed in some form."

"Why videos? Why not just conduct your sessions?" I wondered how accurate it was to call them "his" sessions. I wondered what he thought about, rambling instructions that resulted in activities in which he had no other part, activities that might be considered kinky.

"Ironically enough, it was Arabella who made me consider it. I knew as soon as I met her that she'd take me in a new direction. She'd been in a number of films, and she taught me a lot."

"So Arabella suggested making the videos?" I felt a chill, discussing her. After last night, hearing her name was like touching a Pandora's box of memories and speculations.

"Suggested? I don't know. But the idea arrived with her. I realized my observations would be easier for people to accept if they were on a screen. Rather than tell someone, 'You're not enjoying your sexuality because you're using it to try to assuage and flatter others,' I'd make a tape of that person being fondled and caressed. I'd animate-in auras working like frantic little butlers, trying to please her partner. Simultaneously, they'd be creating discomfort for her.

Or, if two people were making love and one got selfish, I'd make his aura huge and infantile. Nothing fancy—especially at first. But I realized I was dealing with a generation that took its notions of reality from the television screen. They learn more readily by icon and image than by word. I don't think that's a bad thing. It just is. I thank Arabella for showing me that."

"Is she bitter toward you? Does she believe you used her just to get your videos made? Or that you were making some kind of statement when you reimaged her?"

"No, no. She understood what was important. Or so I thought." He turned so we were face-to-face, very close together. "The main thing is to take the technology farther. There's so much to create and explore. The kind of future being made possible now—it will change us as a species. It's that dramatic. Truly."

"Change us in what way?"

"Imagine a holographic, totally three-dimensional reality in which literally anything you think of can happen—that's where the technology is heading."

"We've always had our imagination." I shrugged.

"But now we'll unlock it, we'll free it. We'll make it as close to physical as anything else you perceive. We'll blur the lines: What's quote-unquote real, what isn't? Is this reality"—he waved his arm to indicate the tranquil landscape—"a hologram, as well? Projected from where? By what? Our whole way of thinking about mind and matter will change. We'll finally have to abandon our rigid preconceptions about spirit."

People disposed to think in those terms would continue to do so, and people not so disposed, wouldn't. I didn't see how holographic video games would change that.

To my unspoken skepticism, he replied, "How could it not happen? How could it not change everything?" He placed an earnest hand on my arm. "That's why my work is so important. The closer I get to constructing a new reality, the closer we all get to understanding what's behind this one. That's why my devotees are with me. That's why I'm pushing the technology. For them, for me, for Arabella. She understood that. I thought."

His shoulders drooped. "How sad what happened to those women. I won't—I don't want to use it against Arabella that she's a sex worker. I don't want that to be a defense or whatever. I agree with sex workers' advocacy of tolerance and open-mindedness. I don't want to stand on them to make myself look taller."

"Have you been to The Back Door?"

He nodded. "After-hours with Arabella. So she could film some of her friends."

"I meant for the shows."

"No."

"To me, it looked less like a political statement than a very difficult and exploitative job."

"But to single out sex work for censure and criminalization is . . ."

"Is a separate issue. But I agree with you. And as I said, I don't know if Arabella's work will become relevant. I don't even know for a fact she'll go through with suing you."

"The Rs brought another letter from her lawyer this morning. She's demanding the masters of my videos."

I tried not to look happy. If this turned into a case, it might be emotionally trying. But it would pay the bills. "Don't send them. If they sue, they can subpoena them. I'll want a copy of the letter. And I'd like copies of the unchanged tapes, and copies of every changed version you have. But I'll send you a comprehensive list of what I need."

He blinked rapidly, looking a little overwhelmed. "I'll have the Rs take care of you."

I wasn't sure I'd heard him correctly. But as long as someone took care of me, it didn't matter.

"What else can you tell me about Arabella de Janeiro?"

"Well, in terms of her impact on the group, she touched a nerve. I won't say I'm an ascetic or anything like that, but my own orientation is more, I don't know, call it ephemeral. I hadn't focused much on sexuality." He leaned closer, as if mere eye contact were not enough. "But of course I grew up in this culture, I saw all the magazines, a few of the classic X movies. I could feel people's desires, all that energy under there, under the surface. Even before Arabella came along, I knew it was something to be addressed." He looked suddenly disconcerted. "You've heard of water witches?"

"Yes."

"That's how I think of myself sometimes. When I'm with people, I pick up things about them. I divine their energies—their intellectual and emotional motivations—especially the dark ones, the quote-unquote crazy ones. I don't mean to sound grandiose—I've worked at suspending judgment and remaining attuned. I'll sit with people and listen awhile and find I know what they want and dread, what they're ashamed of or want to act out. Especially—although they might not know this—what they want to get free of."

"To what do you attribute this . . . gift?" I hoped I wasn't going to hear some story of cosmic or religious rebirth.

"Subatomic physics," he said simply. "We recognize the existence of certain waves—like magnetism—by the effects they have on surrounding matter. Well"—he shrugged—"it seems obvious to me that if I'm picking up these energies from people, then the energies are, first off, being broadcast. And, just as obviously, that I'm open to and able to receive them. Beyond that, I'd just be guessing."

"How many of the sexual sessions have you done?"

"Oh, my. When I was still down in San Francisco, we were doing them twice a day sometimes. For months. Like I said, Arabella was part of the impetus, but a lot of other people fed into it. By the time we got into the filming, I was coming up here three, four days a week to clear my head. I was shorting out, you might say." He looked tired just talking about it. "Having devotees is like any relationship. At times, you're immersed. When it fatigues you, you worry that you've become crazy in exact complement to your partner. So you take a step back. Until you can reconnect without that fear."

"Did your devotees pay for this place?"

He nodded, putting a gentle finger behind my elbow to cue me to continue walking. Past the rose orchard the ground sloped, commanding a view of jade islands in a flat sterling sea. A few scant acres, ending in sea-lapped rock, were dotted with hive-shaped structures, some of them topped with antennas.

"I didn't have a cent of my own, really," he continued. "Never did have. I went through college on scholarships. By the time I graduated, a few people pooled together on their own to pay my expenses. Good people." He smiled fondly. "I grew a lot with them. I suspect I come across as the absentminded-professor type. I've been lucky to be surrounded by people willing to take care of my material details."

"So people chip in for your support?"

He nodded, stuffing his hands into his slacks pockets.

"What are all those structures? With the antennas?"

"Receivers. Some transmitters."

"What are you receiving and transmitting?"

"Maybe nothing." He spoke as if slamming a door. "I don't really like to talk about that level of my work. I don't discuss it with my people. It has nothing to do with the sessions or the videos."

"All right." Get flaky on me. "I'd like to talk to you about your reimaging. I'd like to see where and how and to what extent you do it."

He flashed me a huge grin. "With pleasure. We'll do that right now, if you want."

"Fine."

He took my arm, turning us back toward the house. We walked in silence. He was certainly more amiable than I'd expected, less posturing, less preachy. But support him? It was hard to imagine people in the cynical nineties wanting to support a man of mere ideas.

As if in reply to my thought, he said, "It's because of the water-witching aspect, not the ideas. That's what I've grown to think."

"I don't understand what you mean."

"Well, you, for instance. You put your sexuality into other things, things of a highly competitive nature. So you tend to exercise the physical part of the drive in less competitive arenas. No, no, don't take it wrong: I'm not calling you an unsexed woman. If anything, I'd call you a sexy lawyer. But in terms of your sexual alliances, I'd guess you gravitate toward damaged or unsuccessful men: maybe younger, less accomplished, handicapped. Because the heart of your sexual energy is in competition and achievement. Maybe your earliest sexual relationship left you feeling powerless and degraded, and now you put your energy into being on top."

I stopped walking. "I'm not your devotee," I said carefully. "I will not discuss my sexuality or any part of my personality with you unless you feel it bears on my ability to represent you."

"You're angry." He sounded surprised. "But I was only showing you what I mean. About the witching."

"And I'm telling you: you're apparently in the habit of a certain level of instant intimacy. Well, ours is not that kind of relationship. I'm your lawyer. You've drawn conclusions from my demeanor and my reputation, and your conclusions are dead wrong. But even if they weren't—"

"You know, if you'd like to sit in on any of the sessions here this weekend, you could get free of some of the—"

"I don't need to get free. Certainly not of my ambition." Goddamn it. How many variations were there on the old "All you need is a good screw"?

Were his people so desperate for attention they believed his spot analyses? Were they like needy horoscope readers, comforted by the ersatz-personal and blind to the generality?

"I was just trying to explain . . ." He sighed. "You don't have to participate, but you're welcome to sit in on the sessions."

"Do you have anything going on of a nonsexual nature?"

"I wish. But lately, that's what people come to me for. I sometimes think if they don't find a cure for AIDS, this decade will become the craziest in the history of the planet. People's sexuality is festering right into psychosis."

A heavy statement for a man with a degree in . . . in what? "What did you study in college?"

"Physics. I started out in mathematics, but I found it merely descriptive and predictive: you track phenomena by numeric progression, hoping some emerging pattern will enable you to make predictions. That kind of approach is just reportage on an abstract level. But physics—on the subatomic level, most purely—is philosophy, theosophy, poetry. It's where the real debate is, where the best chance of discovering God is. If we can ever understand the photon, we'll know God."

I wasn't holding my breath. I didn't need—and wouldn't trust—that knowledge, anyway. "Do your theories on sexuality track current psychological thought?"

He looked surprised, brows ingenuously raised. "I don't know. I've never checked."

"You give a lot of advice. You experiment with techniques that could be called therapy. Your lack of training and credentials might become an issue now that you're distributing videos."

"But all I do is turn a mirror on people," he protested. "I tell them—or now, with the videos, I show them—what I see in them, what I see coming out of them. I suggest ways to free themselves to explore new concepts. The emphasis on sexuality was more their choice than mine."

I wondered if his passivity would play well to a jury. After watching the videos, hearing what he'd instructed his followers to do, I wasn't impressed by it.

Still, I'd expected a lecherous spouter of pompous love talk. Brother Mike was a pleasant surprise in that regard.

"Why did you decide to market the videos?"

"Money," he said simply. "My equipment costs a fortune—more than this island, if you can believe that. It's such new technology.

Truly magic stuff, but outrageously expensive. My accountant was the one who suggested distributing the videos. Something about having non-gift income to use as the basis for credit for the stuff I'm going to buy next. I figure, if it makes sense to him, fine. If it gets me a Cray XMP and a couple of Sun Stations, fine. From my point of view, the videos were crucial because they taught me how to communicate, especially, as I said, to the television generation. The medium itself has limitless potential—and I mean that literally. And the videos gave me footage to experiment with; making spectral changes, adding auras and animation, three-dimensionality. You're not technically supposed to use film you didn't shoot yourself; it's copyrighted, I'm told. And also the videos got me into reimaging, so that no one would be recognized. Those techniques opened a world of technology to me."

"I recognized Gretchen Miller."

"She had me change her back. She wants the ax to fall."

"What do you mean?"

His look was almost pitying, as if he spoke to a mentally impaired person. "Her law firm will find some excuse to fire her, don't you think? As soon as someone tells them about the video."

"That's probably true."

"She can come here, if she wants." He didn't sound as if he cared much one way or the other. "Wait till I show you my video puppeteering equipment. It's still in its infancy, but I've got some ideas . . ." He looked at me, his face aglow.

For the first time that afternoon, he looked crazy enough to be a preacher.

I finally asked the question uppermost on my mind. "What can you tell me about Margaret Lenin?"

"Margaret?" He raised his graying brows. "Gretchen told me she was okay with all this now. Isn't that right?"

"I thought some insight into her . . . complaints would be useful. Have you heard from her or seen her lately?"

He shook his head. "I don't remember. Maybe the last time I was in the city. The Rs could tell you."

"So she hasn't phoned recently? To your knowledge? You haven't spoken with her or counseled her?"

"No." Then, with an Igor accent, "Won't you join me in my laboratory?"

MY ROOM was an eight-by-eight square with unadorned blue walls, a bed scratchy with army blankets, and a tiny table and chair under the sole window. I flopped onto the bed. I'd spent two hours in a huge basement jammed with color monitors, televisions, "frame-accurate" videocassette recorders, oscilloscopes, and a slough of things that had to be identified for me: digitizing boards, CD-ROM players, timegraph editors, transparency (and at least three other types of) scanners.

For two hours I'd watched Brother Mike hop from electronic sketch pad to keyboard to VCR showing me ways to turn film stills and drawings and geometric shapes into three-dimensional graphics. He added grid lines that fanned around objects like wire exoskeletons. He displayed menus of colors and textures, wrapping his choices over the skeletal frames. He rotated the "texture-mapped" forms, changing the intensity and location of the light source, the angle of the "virtual camera." He created motion by "front-projecting" reflections of passing surroundings, adding "motion blur" as they picked up speed. But the most interesting part of the demonstration (to me, that is; Brother Mike seemed to enjoy every minute of it) was computer puppeteering. He laser-scanned human images onto the computer screen, moving them around by sticking his hands into and rotating the concentric half-spheres of something called a Waldo Motion Device.

It was also interesting to watch him change videotaped faces one frame at a time. He did this a few different ways, from building grids over cheeks and chins and "painting" on textures and colors to grabbing part of a face—an eyelid, for example—and pulling it lower or higher, retouching as necessary with colors and textures taken from surrounding skin. He could make two pictures merge or "morph" into one another, selecting in advance the percentage of each to remain in the final product. He even had department-store software that altered makeup and hairstyles.

I didn't understand much of the patter accompanying his manic two-hour demonstration. It didn't matter. If it became necessary, I'd learn. I'd seen hundreds of thousands of dollars' worth of equipment, though. That interested me. I'd seen gorgeous graphics and impressive animation. I'd watched faces change and move. But it hadn't looked like life, not quite. Some images were too slick and fluid, like entries in an animation festival. Others were just jerky enough to appear unnatural.

But I supposed Brother Mike could do better than the quick, probably elementary stuff he'd shown me. Perhaps I'd see his prowess in the videos he'd made for his followers.

Right now, I didn't care. Right now, I just wanted to be alone.

I'd spoken on the phone to Sandy. His call brought the welcome enervation of relief: Margaret was alive. Margaret was fine. Margaret had gone to work early this morning; had been sitting at her desk at Graystone while I pounded on her apartment door.

That being the case, she must have calmed down last night after phoning me; must have gone home and gone to sleep, not realizing she'd sent me out in the middle of the night.

At least, that's what I assumed. For the sake of a couple of hours' nap, a brief draft of tranquillity, that's what I chose to believe.

Tomorrow I'd talk to Margaret. Right now, I'd relax.

My client had reminded me at least six times that there would be a "workshop" that evening. I knew I should go. But Brother Mike's facile and fallacious, even sexist, analysis of me had been off-putting, to say the least.

And I was sick of being with people.

I stretched out on the bed and closed my eyes.

I lay there for a couple of hours, lights off, trying not to think. Then I reluctantly roused myself to go to Brother Mike's session. I couldn't justify wasting an opportunity to observe his techniques firsthand. If I was going to get prudish, I had no business taking his money.

I couldn't possibly have been any grumpier as I made my way down the oak stairs. It was a cold, damp night. Condensation beaded on every window I passed—no need for curtains when yours is the only house on an island.

Two of Brother's devotees stood at the foot of the stairs, apparently discussing me.

A tall, lank-haired man in his thirties was saying to a short pear-shaped brunette, "She's supposed to be like a superlawyer—she'll take care of Arabella. Let it go."

"Well, it's not that big a deal for you, Roy, but I've got kids and about fifty other relatives. I don't need a ton of publicity about *The Energy of Bondage*."

He nodded as if he'd heard her say so many times.

"What if a list of who's in the videos gets printed in the paper or something?" she continued.

He put a reassuring hand on her shoulder. "Why would it?"

"If it gets to be part of a court proceeding, it's public record. I think."

"Probably she'll drop the whole thing. But you were beautiful, you know? I mean, let's face it, the whole point was to open yourself up. Don't let Arabella shut you down, Rhonda."

"Like I said, Roy"—her voice was steely—"it's not such a big deal for you."

"Maybe not, but maybe it'll do us all good to come out of the closet, in a sense. It's like the Freemasons had all these secret rituals during Catholicism because it wasn't okay to be a free thinker. We're kind of like that now—free thinkers. That's not a disgrace. Arabella's outing us, in a way. Like Queer Nation was doing to famous gay people."

"But what's her agenda?" Rhonda's voice rose in pitch. "First she gets a whole bunch of people hot on the idea of videotaping, which I never liked the idea of in the first place—"

Roy spotted me standing on the stair pretending to look out the window. "Are you Laura?" he asked.

"Laura Di Palma."

"Has a legal case been filed yet?"

"Not to my knowledge."

Rhonda turned away, but not before I saw her painful flush.

"My name's Roy, this is Rhonda. We live here pretty much year round. If Mike goes to San Francisco for more than a week or so, we go down with him."

"You don't call him Brother Mike?"

Roy grinned. "He hates that. But you know people. They keep wanting to give him a title. It's better than 'Oh Exalted Mighty One,' I guess. I suggested Brother. Kind of sounded like a monk. Kind of Russian."

"So you lived with him before he moved here?"

"Yup—I'm head cyberpunk around here. Well, maybe cyberhippie's more accurate. Anyway, yeah. Mike still stays down in the city part of the time. If he goes down to buy machines, usually I go, too. Unless I'm elbow-deep in videotape or computer guts. Or frame-by-frame changes, which are majorly time-consuming—there are thirty video frames a second, so you can imagine."

"Does he go down to the city often?"

"Not too much anymore. He gets overrun. He needs space to think. Rhonda grew up around here; she knew this place. When one of Mike's people offered it, we grabbed it."

I made a mental note to examine the deed; find out the form of ownership.

"I overheard you talking about Arabella."

"Arabella, yeah. Heavy energy around sex." He shook his head, but there was an appreciative glint in his eye.

"Did you know she was beaten up before work last night?"

"No." Roy stood very still. "Did you know that, Rhon?"

She shook her head slowly. "Is she all right?"

"Yes. But quite battered, apparently. You didn't know anything about it?"

Both said no. Both remained motionless.

"Any guesses who might have done it?"

Rhonda ran a thick-fingered hand through her hair. "It's not the best neighborhood."

Had I mentioned where Arabella was attacked?

"You heard about the six employees being killed?"

"Yes. We definitely heard about that."

But they hadn't wondered if one of the women was Arabella?

As if divining my thought, Roy said, "The news tonight listed their names."

I wondered if they'd passed the information on to their guru.

"Did you know any of them?"

"Just barely. Pretty awful." Roy's shoulders climbed. "Crappy way to die. I'd take almost anything over suffocation."

I must have looked surprised.

"I almost drowned when I was a kid. I hate the feeling of not getting enough air."

I supposed Rhonda did, too. She turned away with a shudder.

I had to change the topic before I visualized it.

"I heard you say Arabella shifted the group's focus?"

"That she did." A slight frown creased Roy's forehead. "Rhonda was thinking she changed the dynamic, you know, from more of a head trip to a sex thing. But Mike said that was okay—the thing's got to be fluid and change to suit who's around, like a good conversation. That's what a religion should be."

"You consider this a religion?"

He nodded emphatically. "I came here from Da Love–Ananda. You know, the Great Tradition. I think Mike's one of the incarnations. He doesn't like that vocabulary, but it's definitely what we feel from him."

"Do you agree?" I asked the face-averted Rhonda.

She glanced at me, glanced away, then seemed to force herself to imitate Brother Mike's eye-contact shtick. "I think that's why we're all here, really. What we see in Mike is something we've never seen in any other living creature."

"Da Love–Ananda's cool," Roy interjected. "There's more than one incarnation, some generations."

Rhonda nodded. Her round, thick-browed face was paling almost to normal hue. "It's not that we think he's the only wise man on earth or anything like that. But he is truly wise. He can cut right to the core of you like within minutes of meeting you. It's like his insight comes from someplace special that most people never start to get to."

"Is that what you do here? Try to get to that place?" I felt silly even speaking in those terms.

"Yes. We want to grow from his insights into us and what they teach us about ourselves and the world and the spirit. And we also want to get closer to his place of being able to see into people—"

"And concepts. He sees into ideas. Whether they're bullshit or not."

Again Rhonda agreed with Roy. "Once you know him, you can't leave him. He's like a conduit to higher consciousness, to true insight."

"He's a physics and computer genius," Roy added. "A lot of us here have that background."

Rhonda nodded. "But to go beyond a certain level of understanding, you have to access a different part of your consciousness.

That's what's superdeveloped in Mike. That's the part that Roy would call god-consciousness."

"What do you call it?" I wondered.

"A window into the psycho-physical. Into the future."

A voice called out, "We're set up, Rs."

"Are you coming to the session?" Roy sounded dubious.

Rhonda said, "Unless you plan to fully participate, I'm not sure it's a good idea. It'll make people shy." Her flush returned. It would obviously make her shy.

"Brother—Mike urged me to attend."

Rhonda turned away as Roy said, "In that case." He slipped his arm casually around my shoulders and began squiring me down the corridor.

I wanted to bat his arm away. I wanted to flee now, before I had to see in person what I'd seen on the videos.

"Do you know Margaret Lenin?"

His grin was a little smug. He'd had intercourse with her, probably often; that was my interpretation. But that was probably true of most of the women in Brother's circle. "Haven't talked to her in a while, but sure."

We'd reached an open doorway. I glimpsed a circle of people on cushions.

I preceded "the Rs" into the room, trying to comport myself with surface sangfroid. I regretted my decision almost immediately, as others in the room began eyeing (or maybe I imagined this) my body.

Brother Mike was sitting in a rattan rocker. Over his cardigan, a leather harness anchored a video camera to his chest just below his left shoulder. He wore horn-rim glasses, making him look even more like a nerdy engineer. He motioned me to a stool in the corner, a good fifteen feet from the circle.

Roy closed the door behind us and dropped onto an unoccupied cushion. Rhonda settled in beside him.

I looked the group over. They seemed to be in their thirties and forties, most of them. Two men sported ponytails. One woman had sixties' natural hair and another had a multicolored razor cut. The others looked like urban professionals, with tidy haircuts and Eddie Bauer clothes.

No one in the room was extraordinarily attractive or unattractive. They might have been chosen at random from a Seattle bookstore.

Brother Mike squinted into the camera's periscopic eyepiece. He said, "We've got a group of go-slowers tonight."

The people regarded each other warily, I thought.

"We've got a group of people into holding back the energy until they know damn well what they're going to get in return; that's what I'm feeling." Brother stood, beginning a slow prowl. The camera on his chest made a faint whirring sound.

A few members of the circle hung their heads, a few grinned sheepishly. They seemed to agree. But then, couldn't he have said the same about most groups? Wasn't that life in the nineties?

"So I guess we'll have to go with that energy." He sounded sad about it. "We'll have to do some bartering, get the whole thing out on the table. How about, as a starting proposition, men get sucked after every woman in here has been licked?"

Even though I'd seen his videotapes, his bluntness startled me. I didn't think I'd be able to sit through this. Not after last night.

"Licked to orgasm, I mean." He knelt, camera close to the devotees' faces. "That seems fair, doesn't it? Commercially viable, right?"

Around the circle, everyone froze for a moment. Then a woman smiled. A man laughed. Brother rose, turning slowly to capture reactions.

"Doesn't that seem fair?" he asked again, as if he badly needed the validation of their agreement.

A few people said yes.

I made myself stay, but it wasn't easy. It was an endless ninety minutes of increasingly more elaborate "bargains," announced and discussed at philosophic length by the guru. Roy and Rhonda acted as facilitators, breaking the ice with their instant compliance. Brother Mike, leaning nimbly close or hovering overhead, collected video images.

It was too much. The embarrassment that was notably absent from the group—I seemed to endure all of it. My clothes were soaked with sweat and I felt almost battered. The smell of sex was heavy in the room.

And no one used condoms. I wondered whether I was watching these people's "liberation" or their infection.

The whole thing gave me the creeps. What was worse: it aroused me. That was the part I hated most.

When Brother Mike congratulated them on how well they'd "explored their energy," I slipped out of the room and dashed back upstairs.

I needed to be alone. I needed to get some perspective on what I'd witnessed before I could talk to my client—or anyone else—about it.

17

WHEN I HEARD the knock at my door a half hour later, I considered ignoring it. I'd taken a quick shower and changed into my bulkiest, least-sexy sweater. I felt as if I'd been stuffing my face with fudge, as if I'd overindulged in something cloyingly bad for me.

Afraid more might be required of me as guest or lawyer, I reluctantly opened the door.

It was Brother Mike himself, beaming, rather disheveled, still looking like an absentminded math professor. "Well, that went pretty well, don't you think?"

"I guess that depends on what you were trying to accomplish." My tone was cold.

He didn't seem to notice. He stepped into my room. "I'd have come right up to talk to you, but I often get excited. One of the women helps me out."

I took an appalled step backward. Reminded myself that sex was the background against which this lawsuit would be played. If I couldn't hear my client speak frankly, I wouldn't make it as his lawyer.

I remembered how difficult it had been dealing with my craziest client, Wallace Bean, who'd shot two United States senators. And yet Bean, influenced by Clint Eastwood and Charles Bronson movies, had seemed more mainstream American—and therefore easier to understand—than Brother Mike. His outlook had been mass culture minus a few IQ points and minus the ability to perceive movies as feel-good fantasies, not how-to manuals. Mike Hover was another matter. His meshing of cerebral and carnal was disturbing, almost disgusting. I'd have to work on that, in myself and in my legal presentation of him.

"So, tell me"—I managed to sound professional—"was this session typical?"

He nodded, grinning. "That's why I came up. I was so pleased. I was afraid you'd see something atypical. Like one time, the group got thrown off by someone remembering an early traumatic experience. She got very hostile and wild."

"What did you do?"

He looked surprised. "We took her out of the group. But the energy lingered, it was so intense. There was a victimized feeling from the group that wasn't a real part of its dynamic. I couldn't work with it. For example, the woman I'm talking about, when I got her into a group of people who'd been sexually abused, we both did fine with that energy. But the way she left her mark on the other group . . ." He shook his head. "It just didn't work."

"So you prescreen your groups? For similar . . ." I couldn't quite think what to call it.

"Not prescreen. Every once in a while, I ask someone to leave and come back later when there's a more compatible group. Usually, you know, it's more a question of what's predominant in the group. For the tapes, we set up specialty groups." He plunked himself onto a chair. "It made for better movies."

"How did you prescreen? How did you guard against someone being wrong for the group?"

"They'd all done it with me before. I just shuffled them into the right groups and did the videotaping. Pretty bland stuff. But I did some interesting things with it later. I'll have the Rs give you those tapes. The ones at the video rental places, those aren't any fun. Those are for seed money."

He slumped, crossing his foot over his knee and tapping it lightly with his finger. "There are a lot of hard feelings here toward Arabella."

"I've heard some murmurs."

"From Rhonda? Well, Arabella couldn't have sexualized us if we weren't ready for it. She's one of these people that when she walks into a room, the whole room feels different."

"From my limited observation, it seems you analyze things almost exclusively according to sexual 'energies.'" I failed to keep the word out of aural quotation marks.

He suddenly sat very straight, his face alight. He looked like a happy child. "I know what would work for you sexually."

"No."

"If you—"

"If you go any farther, I will leave and you can find yourself another lawyer. It was useful to me to observe your session, so I did. There was nothing personal about it. This is a business relationship and I will not discuss my private life."

"But if it helped you—"

"Do you want me to continue as your lawyer?"

"Yes."

"Then we don't talk about me."

His head tilted and his eyelids drooped. He looked like a mathematician squinting at a calculus equation. "This is rare. I rarely have premonitions. But I trust them."

"Is this premonition about the case?"

"No. I mean, I don't know what it's 'about,' in that sense. It's about you."

I took a backward step, putting a little more distance between me and this man. He could persuade people—yuppie lawyers, even—to have sex on film, films intended for distribution. I'd lived in San Francisco during the Jim Jones years. I mistrusted that kind of charisma, mistrusted those who held others in their sway.

I'd have to be careful. If I let him share his premonition, I might, to some small degree, accept it and help fulfill it. If I refused to hear it, I bowed to superstition and disquiet.

"Just to be clear," I spoke slowly, "I regard this as a professional relationship. To the extent that who you are is part of the case, then yes, even your premonitions are germane. Not for their content, but as an insight into your mental process."

He grinned. "It must drive your loved ones crazy to have you be so measured and precise on the outside and so chaotic in what you actually end up doing."

I was about to object: I'd stayed on track; my career and reputation were intact. But I considered my elopement shortly after my eighteenth birthday. The way I left town without a word when my marriage broke up. More recently, the way I'd chucked Sandy for Hal without discussion, fallen for Ted McGuin though we had little in common.

"That's depends on how you look at it," I replied. "You could say that to anyone and leave it to them to find it applicable."

"I wonder. I'll have to think about that." He rose, stretching. "Well, I have a lot of confidence in you. I think you'll take care of it just right."

"Take care of what?"

"But I won't." He looked as if something had surprised him, as if he were viewing some internal movie. "You watched one of your clients die."

I felt my stomach knot. Dan Crosetti, who'd deserved a lot more from life. "Yes. It was in all the newspapers."

"Was it? It was very hard on you; it closed up a big place inside you. That's too bad. Try to remember that what you're feeling is magnified extremely by the previous trauma. Try to separate that out so you can fix on the important detail." He shook his head. "I can't quite grab it, whatever it is. But you'll notice it if you can stay focused."

He walked past me, making the kind of sounds a person makes when he's reading something interesting. "Funny—I keep thinking it has to do with me, too. But I can't quite feel how."

It wasn't until he was out the door that he said, "If I don't see you . . . You should have sex with someone who—"

"Stop," I warned him.

"Right." With a grin, he added, "Force of habit."

If he hadn't turned and walked away, whistling absently, I'd have verbalized my anger.

As it was, I slammed the door. I'd told him plainly my private life was off-limits. His assessment was asinine—of course, since he didn't know me. What angered me was the gall of it: giving advice without information. Urging people to act on his guesses. Just because he had the gift—maybe it was as ingenuous as it seemed and maybe it wasn't—of sounding as if he *knew*.

I'd rather make my own mistakes than be right by another's decree.

Lucky thing.

THE NEXT MORNING, a member of last night's session rapped at my partially open door. It was eight-fifteen. I was showered and dressed, about to go in search of coffee.

The man was well-groomed in a polo shirt and Dockers jeans, probably in his late thirties. He had the pleased look of a handsome man and seemed to expect some grateful flirtation from me. But my attitude was colored by what I'd seen in him last night: a preference for being rough and (even under those circumstances) unromantic. I tried to overcome my aversion; this was something about him I had no right to know.

"What can I do for you?" I asked him.

"Brother Mike asked me to bring you to his room."

"All right." The sooner the better. I had an afternoon flight out, and it would take me most of the morning to ferry to the mainland and ride the airporter down to Seattle.

"I'll show you where it is." He stood back to let me exit.

We started down the hall, passing a group of people clustered beside a window. I flashed on what I'd seen them do the night before.

It was awful. It was like being in a household where every person was a former lover. I knew and could visualize too much about each of them. My reaction was almost physical; I felt a little sick.

My escort stopped at a big door, painted blue. "This is it, but . . ."

"Yes?"

"I know about the problems with Arabella and all that. I know you're a lawyer. I am, too," he added with an in-group grin.

Did he expect congratulations? Hail fellow, well met? I waited.

He looked over my shoulder, not meeting my eye. "I was in a couple of videos with her." A quick glance to see if I was impressed. "I got to know her. And the other girls."

I tried to feel sympathy. He'd known the dead women. Maybe he'd cared for them. In any case, the death of six acquaintances would be shocking.

But he seemed to expect a particular response. And I didn't know what it was.

"We even filmed some videos at The Back Door after closing. That was"—a half-smile—"interesting."

"Who's 'we'?"

"Me and another man and Brother Mike and the girls. Man . . ." He cupped his hands over imaginary breasts.

There was little sympathy in his manner, little acknowledgment that people—not just "girls"—had died. "The women were devotees?"

"Them? God, no." His smirk was indecorous at best.

Lawyers are trained to be conventional in their social expression. What did his tone mean? That the women, because of Arabella's lawsuit, had become enemies of the commune?

"We were only there twenty minutes, half an hour, at a time," he continued. "I think it was more a favor to Arabella. She was into filming them with us."

"Did they sign releases?" The one signed by Margaret Lenin warned participants that the videos might be distributed for public viewing. Signatories consented to "any use or alteration of images contained therein, for commercial or any other purposes" without expectation of payment.

"No, it was more on a horsing-around level. Arabella took a few of us over there a couple of nights and Brother Mike brought the camera. He wasn't doing sessions or anything. Arabella mentioned she'd taken home movies—that's what she called them—for him before. But the point I'm trying to make is, I do know her."

I interpreted his grin as stupidly lascivious. Perhaps the reaction was unfair. It was freighted with years of disdain for certain kinds of men, men with clichéd suppositions about what women wanted and liked. Dumb men in bars. Full-of-themselves jocks in lawyer suits.

"Anyway, the reason I bring this up: if I can be of any help to you . . ." He extracted a business card from his shirt pocket. "I do know her. Rather well." He left little doubt as to what "rather well" meant.

I took his card. A maritime lawyer. Some help he'd be.

I knocked at Mike Hover's door.

He called out, "Who is it?"

I answered.

"If you're alone, come in."

I glanced behind me, waiting for the lawyer to leave. He looked disappointed. But he turned and walked away.

I stepped into a corner room of little wall and many windows. Light from the white-sky morning showed a chill, austere space with a cluttered desk, an easy chair, and a small four-poster bed.

I wanted to focus on the decor of the room, on the view from the window. I didn't want to focus on Brother Mike, handcuffed hand and foot to the posts of the bed, a loose black cowl over his face, not a stitch of clothing on his thin, out-of-shape body.

"Close the door," he said gently.

This was not working out for me. As much as I wanted a splashy, highly visible case, I couldn't handle all the naked bodies, all the sexual oddity.

I was at a loss for words. I shut the door.

"I'm not quite sure how to get out of these," he said.

"Shall I call Roy?" I wondered if he'd done this to himself or if it had been part of exploring his "energies."

"She took the keys."

Trying not to look down, I yanked a blanket out from under him and covered him. I pulled the cowl from his face. "Are you saying this was involuntary?"

"Well, it was a surprise, if that's what you mean." He was flushed, damp hair sticking to his forehead. "I was sound asleep. One of my hands was shackled before I even woke up."

"And you didn't struggle?"

"I don't suppose I did, I was so much in my dream still. I was dreaming that Arabella—"

"What did you actually see? Or feel or smell?"

"I felt passion and happiness—from the person with the handcuffs, I mean. A true and satisfying and profoundly motivating anger. That's what kept me half in the dream state, I think; I was feeling that from Arabella in the dream, and then I woke up with one hand cuffed and something going over my eyes, I was still feeling this rush of, like I said, the purest joy of anger." He sounded more bewildered than embarrassed. "So I didn't fight. I let her cuff the other hand. I was sharing her exultation."

He surprised me. I didn't regard anger as one of the happier emotions.

A spark of intellectual engagement vivified his expression. "Anger can be very dark and negative and even paralytically caustic in some people," he explained. "People like you, who survive by retaining control. But every once in a while in some people, you see that real American can-do kind of anger. Our films teach it to us, right back from the World War Two musicals to the Rambo movies. To be angry is to be energized. It's the American high. That's why we love alcohol so much; it works well with anger. And anger makes us happy."

I supposed. "Did your attacker say anything to you?"

"Well, I don't know." His tone shifted back into bewilderment. "I was getting such a hit of the energy, I don't remember if any of it was verbalized. I really don't remember."

Damn, he'd make a terrible witness.

"Did you notice any identifying characteristics? The way the hands felt? A kind of perfume? Are you sure it was a woman?"

"No, no. None of the surface stuff. I wasn't tuned into that."

Great. "Well, whoever it was, where did she go? Do you have any idea?" I glanced at the French doors leading to what appeared to be a balcony. "Did she go out this way?"

"I don't know. Like I said, for a couple of minutes I was caught up in her emotions. Then I realized I needed help. I called out and luckily someone was in the hall for me to send after you. But I didn't hear her leave. At a certain point, I just felt she was gone."

I gave the doors a push, stepping onto a small balcony with stairs down to the lawn. Adirondack chairs faced the rail. I ran my hand over one of the arms, wiping away a fine stipple of dew. The seat, I noticed, was dry. I supposed the handcuffer had occupied it, perhaps preparing the cuffs and cowl.

In the meadow below, devotees raised their arms toward the fog-dimmed sun, bending backward, then forward. There was no sign of anyone fleeing.

I stepped back in.

"Why did you call for me?" I examined the shackle securing his pale, crooked-toed foot to the bedpost. His ankle was blue-veined and hairy, small in its chrome loop.

No reply.

"Do you suspect Roy's complicity? Are you afraid he smuggled her in?"

"No, not Roy, not any of my people here. Is the boat in? What time is it?"

"It's eight-thirty; a little later. I don't know anything about a boat. I want to know why you called me."

"It's just that Roy and the rest of them, well, they worry so much."

I wondered if it was worthwhile pressing for a more detailed response.

Close by, a boat blasted its horn.

Brother jerked, cuffs rattling. "Could you go down to the room where we were last night and check in the cedar chest for a universal handcuff key? It looks like a gray pen with a pointy thing on one end and a key part—"

"I know what a handcuff key looks like." I'd seen them on cops' belts. "Why didn't you call for Roy?" I assumed Roy knew the exact location of all their sex props, including handcuff keys.

"I'm a little uncomfortable—my bladder. If you could hurry? We could talk afterward."

I hesitated. It mattered a great deal to me. If part of his agenda was exhibiting himself to me, I'd have to reconsider acting as his counsel.

Except that he was paying me a hefty retainer. And God knew, I could use it.

"Why don't I call Roy now?" I was his lawyer, not his gofer. Maybe it was petty to harp on it, but the fact remained.

"Please," he said, "my bladder's going to explode. And everyone here has so much baggage about my well-being. It's simpler this way. Until I can think it through." A final "Please. If you could hurry?"

Still something nagged at me. Nevertheless, I dashed downstairs, ignoring the curious glances of a threesome in the corridor. They were discussing a tract of land in Oregon that was selling cheap and would accommodate a "serious" tent village. Rajneesh's old place, one said. I didn't recognize them. They hadn't taken part in last night's session. Two had overnight bags at their feet.

I kept my eyes on the shined wood floors, trying to trace the source of my anger. When I got to the room with the cushions, Rhonda appeared beside me.

"Did you leave something in here?"

"I'm on an errand. For Mike. Is the door locked?" I couldn't get it to budge.

She gave it a push. "It shouldn't be. It isn't usually even closed. Hunh."

"Do you have a key for it?"

"I know where the key is, I think. Hold on." She trotted away.

I leaned against the door. Something was wrong. This wasn't following the pattern of any of my previous cases, not even remotely. I told myself the nature of the case precluded similarity, but I couldn't shake a feeling I was being manipulated. Why had Brother Mike called for me?

Roy appeared a few moments later. He too tried the door, saying, "It shouldn't be locked."

"You don't worry about thieves?"

"On an island? Not likely they'll scuba in. Or get away with your stuff, for that matter." He pushed again. "I'll be damned. Rhonda just handed me this. Let's see if it . . ." He fumbled a key into the lock. "There were some in a cupboard when we bought the house. We've never had to use them."

The key turned easily.

"Thanks." I opened the door, feeling the inner knob. A push-in lock. It might have been pressed accidentally. I was surprised it hadn't happened before. "Are there new people here this morning?"

"Yes, a group from San Francisco—the boat came in half an hour ago. What do you need in here?" Roy sounded suspicious. "Rhonda said Mike sent you on an errand."

"Yes, Mike sent me. How many on the boat? Who are they?"

"Like I said, devotees from San Francisco. Six or seven of them."

"You're sure they're all devotees?"

"I don't know them personally. Why? What's wrong?" He clutched my arm.

I pulled free. "I'd keep an eye on them till Mike comes downstairs." I entered the room. "In the meantime, like I said, he sent me down on an errand." I closed the door behind me.

I stood there a moment, expecting Roy to follow. He didn't. I had the guru's endorsement.

The room looked small and bare in the silver light of morning. Cushions piled in the center showed watery stains in the dye. I crossed the polished floor fighting a rush of memories.

There was a cedar chest at the far end, beneath a curtainless window. I squatted in front of it, lifting the lid. As I'd imagined, it was filled with standard sex toys—flimsy leather whips, studded harnesses, leather and satin bindings, handcuffs, some padded, some metal. I hated to touch the stuff. I scanned the cedar bottom until I saw a glint of scored gray steel, then reached in carefully, extracting it from the tangle.

I looked up for a moment, admiring the view from the window. It was so pristine here, the mottling of autumn leaves and evergreens unspoiled by painted houses and littered roads. I gripped the handcuff key and fought a wave of anger. Mike Hover was ruining it as surely as a crass developer. Bringing in all this leather, all these people—he was changing it from the inside out, changing the way I looked at it.

I found Roy lurking in the corridor outside, obviously hoping I'd explain my errand.

I didn't. I dashed back upstairs.

I tapped at Brother Mike's door knowing it was a stupid formality given his inability to open it. Nevertheless, I announced myself before entering.

This too proved a wasted gesture. The room was empty.

I approached the bed. The sheets retained the crumpled concave of recent use, but there was no sign of handcuffs on the posts. A dresser drawer was crookedly open, underwear trailing. The closet door yawned.

The bathroom door was ajar. I stepped in. There were recent splashes on the mirror. The water in the toilet no longer eddied, but hadn't quite returned to stasis. I walked back across the bedroom.

I pushed through the French doors, stepping to the balcony rail. Bracing mist drifted across the island, muting its colors, bringing the cold smell of sea water. Along the horizon, ocean and sky blurred into a silver band.

Close to shore, a motorboat arced through the water, maybe carrying Mike Hover away.

I'd have feared for him if I hadn't seen evidence of his ablutions. As it was, even supposing he hadn't staged the whole thing (and I had no reason to think he hadn't), he was probably in little danger from kidnappers who allowed him to use the facilities first.

I went back downstairs and told Roy he should look for Brother Mike, that he'd been handcuffed to the bed prior to (somehow) leaving his room. Without waiting for Roy to become less agog, I added, "And I'll need you to cut me a retainer check and arrange my boat and car ride to the Seattle airport."

With luck, Mike Hover would turn up before I left. If not, I'd phone from the airport to satisfy my curiosity.

If I learned a crime had been committed, and if I was asked to respond as either a witness or an attorney, I would do so. Until then, I would stick to my original plan.

Mike Hover had plenty of other people to worry about him and look for him.

I just wanted to get back home, to be alone. Unlike Brother Mike's titillated devotees, I liked being the organizing principle behind my reality.

19

BROTHER MIKE had gotten to me. As an attorney, I was supposed to be safe from certain intimacies. Yes, I had cared about some of my clients—I still mourned Dan Crosetti. My pity and my conscience were sometimes vulnerable. But my business suit and my sexual feelings had never been part of the same package.

I sat on the airplane, flying home to San Francisco, feeling discouraged and overmatched. I made two phone calls. The first was to Brother Mike's group. I asked if he'd returned. Roy told me they'd had a call from him.

"Where was he calling from?"

"The mainland."

"He left without telling you?"

"Yes." Roy sounded plenty irritated. "On the boat that brought the devotees over. I guess he heard the fifteen-minute horn—he went running down to the dock with nothing but some cash and plastic. Just like Rhonda thought he would. She should have left him handcuffed till it was gone."

"Rhonda unlocked him?"

"She went up after she talked to you. She's got her own key."

The Energy of Bondage—she'd mentioned being in that video. Apparently it reflected her preferences.

"She unlocked him and left him there? You're sure?" Rhonda

seemed to be second lieutenant; theoretically, she wouldn't lie about freeing her guru. But she was angry about the distribution of the videos. I'd heard her say so to Roy. Maybe angry enough to teach Brother Mike an anonymous lesson. Angry enough to have him abducted?

"What am I going to tell everyone? Damn it."

"The people who arrived this morning, they're definitely devotees?"

"I don't know them personally. But why else would anyone come all this way?"

To handcuff a guru to his bed? To collude in a kidnapping?

"Is the boat one of yours?"

"No. It's from a charter place on the big island. I don't know what I'm supposed to do with the devotees. They're expecting a session this afternoon."

"Did you ask Mike when he called?"

"I didn't take the message or I'd have told him to get his butt back here. But maybe Rhonda's right . . ." He paused.

"Rhonda took the message?"

"No, Jeff did."

"Is Jeff one of the new people? You're not taking a stranger's word for this?"

"I think you met Jeff. Kind of a pretty lawyer."

"Do you trust him?" I didn't.

"He's been part of the group quite a while, if that's what you mean."

It was, and it wasn't. "What did he tell you Mike said?"

"He said Mike was laughing. Talking about how politics are nothing but a ball and chain. That Mike was in a real good mood." Roy's tone told me he didn't share that mood. "He's supposed to call back tonight."

The plane dipped over crater lakes the color of rain clouds. A thread of road filigreed the volcanic slope. Evergreens rose in ragged silhouette against a watercolor-gray sky.

"You're sure he won't come back in time for the session?"

"Huh!" Roy's tone bespoke bitter experience. "When Mike pulls this shit, it means shopping. There's a cyberspace show in the valley. Me and Rhonda went and scouted it—definitely a good one. But we *agreed* he'd wait until tomorrow, till everyone left. Okay, so he's a scientist, not a therapist, quote-unquote, piss and moan, and he's got to keep his eye on the future! But what difference is a day going to make? It's not like the future's going anywhere. He's such a kid about moving-holography and VR."

"VR?"

"Virtual reality. Damn it, some of these people have to leave after dinner. We've got a boat coming for them. Which is pretty fucked, considering they paid their own way here."

"They came specifically to make a video?"

"Yes." His tone was decidedly more parental than devotional.

"If you don't get a call tonight—if you don't speak to Mike yourself—let me know." I gave him my home number.

I hung up. I'd known clients to do stranger things. Why did I find this so inscrutable?

Someone, in a "joyous" rush of anger, had handcuffed Brother Mike to his bed.

Once freed, he'd washed his face, then dashed to catch the boat that had ferried in the morning's devotees.

Why the hurry? Because he'd felt the whim to shop and was used to doing as he pleased?

Or had Rhonda been lying? Had the pretty lawyer been lying?

Without more information, it was useless to speculate. It was useless to imagine a connection to The Back Door murders—I begged myself not to, in fact.

My second call, made in don't-think-about-it-anymore haste, was to Arabella de Janeiro's attorney.

It was time to find out what, as well as whom, I was dealing with.

I WAS ACHY and dehydrated after a turbulent and worrisome flight. I was depressed to return to an apartment I still couldn't call "home." I unlocked the door and hit my light switch.

I looked at my living room and turned the light back off. I couldn't have seen what I thought I'd seen. I couldn't have, and so I turned the light off.

I'd watched strange videos lately. I'd sat in on strange shows, stranger sessions. I'd watched them without quite accepting their reality; they had nothing to do with me, not really.

I'd seen seven dead bodies, seen them and scored myself with recriminations for putting myself in a position to see them. I'd run away from seven corpses, taking with me information that might have helped the police. I'd run away from the physical reality of their presence because I hadn't been willing to accept the implications of what I'd seen.

In the dark, for a tiny interval, I tried to reerect the wall of aloof voyeurism that had protected me from three days of sensory overload. But when I turned the light back on, the impossible scene was still before me.

My living room had been torn apart.

Standing there in cold shock, a rational part of me issued commands: Look around. See what's been done, and maybe you'll understand why.

I heeded the voice only because further denial was impossible. I began a slow survey. Everything I encountered had been overturned or displaced or tossed down or spray-painted. The painting was the most shocking. The far wall, a dull beige, was looped with a fuzzy-edged black line. It cut across my collage, coating its lovely hand-made papers.

All the objects Hal had dirtied or not cared enough about, all the objects I'd been waxing and admiring as if they'd give me some of the comfort he hadn't, all those objects had been brutalized. As if to slap me for lavishing attention on mere things.

I stepped farther inside, leaving the door open. I would want to leave soon. I would want to be with Sandy.

Halfway across the living room, I turned around and closed the door. I didn't need to run to anyone. I needed to think; that was more important than solace.

And I'd lied to Sandy. Maybe this had something to do with my lies.

I had to be careful before I shared this with anyone. I had to understand it first. That was the only way to protect myself.

My quick impression, walking through the room, was that someone had been angry. Just angry, not looking for anything. Chairs had been overturned, but cushions weren't scattered or slashed. Hutch drawers had been pulled out and flung to the floor, but their contents seemed strewn only by momentum. I entered the bedroom, steeling myself.

I turned the light on, finding nothing overtly amiss. My body flooded with relief.

My anger thesis might need revision: Had the vandal's anger been sated after only one room? Or was I the object of a warning? Wrecking one room might be enough to make a point.

I backtracked through the living room.

Like the bedroom, the kitchen was untouched.

I walked slowly back through the living room. I'd gotten in the habit, after seeing how Dan Crosetti lived, of viewing my possessions as symbols: of working at White, Sayres & Speck; of putting my energy into having, rather than doing, the right things.

I touched the paint sprayed over my collage, a wonder of textures and colors. It had been on my wall so long my eyes usually ignored it. Now it was traversed by what might have been car touch-up paint. The black line continued across the wall in a messy circle.

I stepped back. A shaky circle with a loop on the bottom.

Maybe not a loop, maybe a cross with its lines connected. Maybe a circle with a cross beneath; the ancient representation of a mirror symbolizing woman.

I staggered back, colliding with an overturned chair.

What did it mean? Something to do with the dead women at The Back Door?

Was the person who'd killed them after me?

Did someone know I'd found the bodies?

I wanted to flee. I wanted to be with someone. I wanted to feel safe.

I forced myself to breathe deeply. I walked to the telephone.

I dialed Sandy's number. He didn't pick up. I left him a message. Please come over. Come now.

I turned away from the paint. I followed pathways chance had left in my living room.

Nothing else had been damaged, only displaced or overturned or flung down.

It had been a quick job, probably. A hurry-through of knocking over and pulling out, with a flourish of paint.

Anger wouldn't look like this if it were personal, would it? If I tore through the room of an individual I hated, I'd dawdle vengefully over things that unpredictably fed my fury. I'd ravage in a more animal and less systematic way. I'd do more real damage.

It was a message, it had to be. Woman. It had to be about the women at The Back Door. Someone knew I'd found them. Or someone wanted to do to me what had been done to them.

Why? Because I'd been there that night? Because I'd seen the show? Because I'd seen something whose significance I didn't fathom?

I wanted to leave this apartment. I hadn't lived here long enough to think of it as mine, anyway. I'd get a new apartment. Now. I had a bag packed from my trip north. I'd just go. Whoever did this wouldn't find me.

Except that I had an office, too. I had a career that made me visible.

Aloud, I realized, "I can't become Hal. I can't hide."

I was no use being a recluse. I'd wasted most of a year and a hell of a lot of money proving that to myself.

I forced myself to look at the situation as it was, unmagnified by recent trauma. (Wasn't that what Brother Mike had counseled me to do? Had predicted I would do?)

The overall effect was shocking, but it would be relatively easy to fix. I'd have to take down the collage and repaint the wall. I'd have to right the furniture and restore the contents of the drawers (worrying as I went along; perhaps that was the point).

This was some kind of war cry. But I could do battle, too.

Whoever had done this had failed to make their point discernible to me. That's what made it scary. But perhaps that reflected their weakness, not their strength.

It had something to do with the dead women. It had to.

But I hadn't killed them, and no one could prove otherwise. I would remain calm.

I'd remove myself from this apartment and I'd be on guard, and no one would hurt me. No one would blackmail me because I'd go to the police myself before I let that happen.

I'd be all right. If I stayed calm.

I sat on the sofa, skewed to a strange position facing the bedroom door.

I could hear Brother Mike's voice in my head: *You'll notice something if you can stay focused.*

He'd told me some vague "it" would happen—a safe-enough prediction—and that my reaction would be distorted by an earlier trauma. He'd advised me to make myself notice something.

It was generic advice applicable to a range of situations. I realized that now. But it was good advice, nevertheless.

I walked back through the living room, looking at everything again. A quick dishevelment; what did it tell me? That this was a hired job, fast and sloppy? Or anger that knew bounds and showed restraint?

A triple ring of the doorbell told me Sandy had arrived.

I opened the door. He was wearing a sport jacket and slacks. He must have arrived home from work and listened to his messages before changing. I was glad he'd come immediately without taking time to call.

"Sandy, look at this and tell me: Should I be scared?" I waved at the damage. "I'm talking myself out of being scared."

"Doesn't mean shit," he replied, beginning his circuit around the room. "Only thing you ever stay scared about is stuff you do yourself."

I didn't reply.

"But maybe that's part of the problem here?" He turned to face me. "Besides the obvious, what are you worried about?"

"Isn't the obvious enough?"

"Yes. But that's not what I'm asking." He tilted his head, his expression hovering between sympathy and distrust.

"I don't know who did this or why." Nonresponsive but true.

He watched me a moment. Then he turned back to the painted circle, touching it with two fingers. "Are we calling the cops?"

I leaned against the wall. What could they do for me? "If I have no idea what this is about, they certainly won't."

"True," he agreed.

"They'll tell me to move out for a while if I'm nervous."

"Also true. But you can get that advice from me."

I headed toward the bedroom to gather more belongings. I'd be ready to go by the time Sandy was through snooping.

I WAS TIRED the next morning. With Sandy's help, I'd moved into a downtown hotel. I had enough clothes to get me through the week, and I'd set the call-forwarding function on my answering machine to ring straight up to my room without going through the desk. Sandy had lent me one of his office machines to pick up on my end, so no one would know I'd left my apartment. No one would know where I was. My only regret was the cost of the room. But I still had some credit. And what else could I do?

I put on a linen blouse and a double-breasted gray suit. I put on gray-white hose and gray shoes. I'd had my hair cut to downplay what my stylist called "the boing factor." I looked like the lawyer I'd always been; and I didn't. Some of the polish and enthusiasm were gone. I'd brought back the smallest hint of country disregard. It was in the absence of silver chains and earrings, it was in the unmoussed hairline and the uncolored nails. Most of all it was in my face. The smooth cordiality of my lawyer mask had cracked slightly. I could see the real emotion beneath; right now, it was fatigued discontent. I'd have to make sure other feelings remained hidden.

I was surprised to hear a knock on the door.

Sandy ran long fingers over his windblown hair. I could tell something was wrong.

I opened the door saying, "What is it?"

"You okay this morning?" He inclined his head, watching me.

"Yes."

"Margaret Lenin phoned in sick today. But she doesn't answer her phone or her doorbell. I'm wondering if she had anything to do with trashing your place. I'm also wondering about the guru. You heard from Hover yet?"

"I told his chief minion to call me last night if he didn't hear from him." I crossed to the telephone. "But let me check and make sure."

I flipped through the Rolodex on the tiny hotel desk. I punched Brother Mike's number into the phone. At first no one answered. Ten or twelve rings later, a sleepy voice said, " 'Lo?"

"Who's speaking?"

"Paulette. Who's this?"

"Laura Di Palma." Which one was Paulette? Had I met her at the session? Was she the big-hipped one who kept moaning when—

"Is Brother Mike back yet?"

"No." It sounded as if her hand had gone over the mouthpiece. I heard muffled speech. "You're the lawyer from San Francisco?"

"Yes. Are you sure he's not there?"

"Uh-huh. We were supposed to have another session and we couldn't. And he was supposed to be at breakfast for a round table this morning and he wasn't. It's not a big deal for me—I live in Port Townsend. But a bunch of people had to go back last night."

"Are Roy and Rhonda there?"

"No. They left. I think they went to get him."

"Went where?"

"The mainland, I guess."

The mainland was a very big place. "Can you get me whoever seems to be in charge right now?"

"Um. Gosh, I'm not sure. Everyone's sort of scattered. I'm not sure where anyone is."

"Look, I need to speak to either Roy or Rhonda immediately. You'll have to go find me someone who can tell me how to reach them." I gave her my apartment phone number, trusting call-forwarding to reroute it here or to my work number. "I need to speak with someone very soon. If you absolutely can't find anyone, call me back anyway."

"I'll try." She sounded too intimidated to do even that much well.

"Is Jeff there? I think that's his name. He's a lawyer from San Francisco."

"I think he went back last night."

I hung up, telling Sandy, "Hover's still gone. His two lieutenants are gone now, too."

I fumbled in my handbag, extracting the maritime lawyer's card.

"Let me try this guy." I dialed the number. To my relief, I got through.

"Hello, this is Laura Di Palma. We met yesterday."

"Of course." The lawyer's voice was warm with innuendo.

I kept my tone frosty. "I'm trying to locate Michael Hover, or, alternatively, Roy or Rhonda. Can you help me?"

"No, sorry. I talked to Brother Mike yesterday. All he said was he was back on the mainland. Roy got pissed off about it—there were some things scheduled. Rhonda was a little more mellow. She basically said, you know, we could trust Brother to do what was most important. But they went after him when he called back."

"He did call back?" I had only this lawyer's word for it. It troubled me.

"Around dinnertime. Roy came in and announced there definitely wouldn't be a session. He and Rhonda left on the same boat we did."

I thanked him and hung up.

"I don't know what the hell's going on." I sat opposite Sandy on a blue floral couch. "Hover and his people are 'on the mainland.' No one's being more specific than that."

He nodded. But his brows were pinched, he wasn't meeting my eye. "I don't like that de Janeiro was pinioned and slugged. It's like someone wanted information. Or assurances. Same with the women at The Back Door. Could be someone was trying to scare them into agreeing to something." He was slumping, legs splayed in front of him. He'd been a cop a long time. Maybe something had struck him; maybe he didn't quite know what.

"I have an appointment with Arabella's attorney this morning," I told him. "I need to hustle."

"Fast work." He didn't sound surprised. "Meet you afterward. Lunch okay?"

"Pick me up at the office. I'll have a check for you."

It pleased me to know I'd see him later.

ARABELLA DE JANEIRO'S attorney looked out of place in a reception area of glass tabletops and Japanese flower arrangements. She was a thick-waisted, somberly dressed woman whose brows met over the bridge of a too-small nose. Her skirt hung long and her blouse gapped. Her brown hair was sheared in front where curls might have been attractive, and long in back, forming a frizzy pyramid that shortened her neck.

I felt a twinge of superiority. It disconcerted me. After my recent night of watching doll-perfect bodies, I hated my gut-level disdain for frumpiness.

She extended her hand. "Hello. I'm Judy Wallach. Come on back to my office." Her voice had an interesting timbre, not deep or loud, but somehow large, a singer's voice.

I followed her through several turns of a corridor, past open doors framing exquisite lawyers in silk shirt sleeves. Their furniture, I noticed, was uniform: mostly old-fashioned oak, stately and oiled. Associates, not partners. Partners would enjoy individualized suites.

"Have a seat." Judy Wallach gestured toward burlap-weave chairs with oak arms. Her office, like her neighbors', was standard and middling expensive.

"About your request for masters of Mike Hover's videos . . ." I smoothed my skirt. Just looking at her made me feel wrinkled. "I'm confused. You haven't stated a cause of action or even indicated an area of contention. Why should my client turn his property over to you?"

A flash of mirth crossed her face. But she didn't actually smile. "I guess I could have been more specific in my demand letter. I assumed you'd know I wanted the masters to check against the distributed copies of the videos."

"Why? Your client signed a release giving up her right to protest any changes in the film or distribution of it."

"A release is only as broad as a reasonable person's understanding of its terms. And not even a highly educated person would know about or foresee the huge technological leaps your client took. The average person doesn't know those types of changes are possible. Arabella de Janeiro did not sign away her right to look like herself because she didn't know it was possible to have her image altered."

"Nonsense. She knows my client intimately; and his love of computer technology is legendary. But even supposing she didn't know, what damages did she suffer? Her privacy hasn't been invaded—she's not recognizable. And she didn't make the films to further her career, so she didn't suffer due to lack of recognition."

"You know my client is an exotic dancer?"

"Yes. I've been to The Back Door."

She put a quick lid on her surprise. "Then you know a dancer's appearance is the basis of her ability to generate income. That's why unauthorized tampering with my client's appearance, especially a wholesale degradation of it, is severely damaging to her self-esteem. And given the nature of her work, lack of confidence can be crippling."

Wallach sat forward, brushing aside file folders and leaning on her forearms. "This is a situation where making a person look less attractive in a commercial context profoundly impacts her career. My client makes her living being beautiful. More than that, she makes her living thinking of herself as beautiful and imparting a certain feeling about herself to others."

"Every devotee of every philosophy is in it to be changed." I knew

I sounded patronizing; that was fine. "If the devotee decides later she didn't like the methods or the results, that may be sad, but it's part of the package. It's hardly the basis of a lawsuit."

"You're assuming my client acted according to the belief system she adopted from your client. That's not the case. He did something later, after her act of devotion, that fundamentally altered it. Altered it in as blatant a manner as I've ever seen." Her cheeks flushed and she fidgeted in her chair. Either she was impassioned on her client's behalf or she was uncomfortable with the details. I knew the feeling. "Michael Hover won his disciples' devotion, then turned around and used them for his amusement. You know he couldn't tamper with other film because of copyright problems. He just wanted video images to manipulate. If he'd been a therapist, there would be no question of his having acted unethically. If he'd been a rabbi, a lawyer, a guidance counselor—"

"Counselors are bound by secular rules of ethics. Religious leaders operate in an entirely different sphere. You can't judge a guru by the same standards as a state-licensed therapist; not without stepping all over religious freedom."

"It's not that simple. Hover doesn't offer a religious package. He offers a type of therapy—in essence, sex therapy." She managed to sound calm and confident, despite her flushed face. Despite the big holes in her theory.

"That is categorically untrue. My client is not a therapist. To say so is to utterly mis-characterize his relationship to his devotees."

"I guess what we have here is a question of fact."

Judges rule on questions of law—the interpretation of statutes, case law, common law. But jurors decide what the facts are. Was Brother Mike a guru or a therapist? Would a reasonable person understand that changes in a videotape might include reimaging? Could such changes result in self-esteem and career damage?

I looked at Judy Wallach, sizing her up. She was making a case out a sow's ear, and she was doing a pretty good job so far. She'd be an interesting opponent.

"Your client's profession will work against her in jurors' minds," I pointed out.

She smiled. "If it turns into a personality contest on that level, your guy stinks."

I was startled. Attorney's don't usually speak so bluntly, not without heat. I'd have to put some time into tracking Wallach's quirks, figuring out how to use them against her.

She was sitting back in her chair now, her look of appraisal probably mirroring mine.

"I heard about the attack on your client. Have you had word about her condition?"

Her brows pinched. "What attack?"

"My information is that she was beaten somewhere near The Back Door at about eight o'clock Tuesday night. On her way to work."

Judy Wallach's hand was already on the telephone. "Please excuse me. I'll need to follow up on that."

"You didn't check on her after what happened"—why be coy?—"after the murders Wednesday morning?"

She held the receiver aloft. "She wasn't a named victim nor, to my knowledge, was she sought for questioning. Or of course I would have spoken with her."

Not sought for questioning: why not? Surely the police wanted to interview everyone who worked there? More likely, de Janeiro hadn't phoned Wallach.

I wished I could speak to someone at Homicide without putting myself in the position of lying to them.

"They're not questioning the deceased women's coworkers?"

"As I said, to my knowledge they haven't contacted my client."

To my knowledge. That meant she'd left messages on de Janeiro's machine, perhaps. Written her a letter.

But she hadn't realized her client was in the hospital. She hadn't been looking for her in the right place.

Her cheeks grew ruddy with consternation. She held the telephone receiver conspicuously aloft, obviously waiting for me to leave.

I sat there another moment, making sure of my dismissal. I'd have preferred to overhear her conversation, to find out the latest. Or maybe I was making a statement: I'm in your space until I choose to leave.

Perhaps lawyer society wasn't that different from baboon society.

She rose and extended her hand. "We'll be in touch," she said.

To remain would be tantamount to breast-beating. I demonstrated my evolutionary superiority. "Thank you for your time."

23

GRETCHEN MILLER'S office was six floors above Judy Wallach's. I found her at liberty.

"Gretchen? Have you seen Margaret Lenin? Or heard from her?" As long as I omitted some details, I could be blunt. "She phoned me Tuesday night in the wee hours. She sounded upset. She said she'd tried to reach you."

Gretchen's face froze.

The night of the murders, Margaret had tried to reach Gretchen, but Gretchen hadn't answered her phone. For the first time, I wondered if that might be significant.

"Are you certain?" Gretchen's tone was cool. But then, I'd burst into her office with this strange query. Who knew what I'd interrupted? "I always leave my message machine on."

"Maybe she didn't want to speak to your machine. Did your phone ring?"

She shrugged. "I didn't waken, if it did."

I was getting bogged down in detail. "Have you spoken to Margaret since?"

"No."

"She was upset because Arabella was beaten up on her way to work. By two men."

"I heard about that from Mike and Roy. Their impression was

that Arabella was basically all right. But they hadn't heard from her. I don't imagine it will affect her decision to sue, do you?"

"I have no idea. I just spoke with her lawyer. She didn't know about the beating."

"Well, it's no use speculating. We'll have to wait." No expression of sympathy. If she'd ever felt friendship for Arabella, it had been erased by the dancer's disloyalty to the guru. "Did you come here to discuss Arabella and Margaret?"

"Only partly." I had, in fact. But it wouldn't do to admit it. I wasn't sure why, but I could see it in Gretchen's stiff posture. "I spent yesterday morning and the day before on Mike Hover's island. I suppose I'm wondering what you get out of your association with him."

"Yes, I knew you'd been up there." She watched me, her face guarded. "I don't quite understand what you're asking."

I was off-kilter, disturbed about something that had—or maybe something that hadn't—been said about Margaret. I was flailingly blunt. "Every organization out there, every religion, every crackpot has an answer. I guess what I'm asking is: Why does this person's answer satisfy you? Did you get tired of questioning?"

"Of course I got tired of questioning." Her facial flush was at odds with the frost in her tone. "That doesn't make me dumb enough to settle for any old answer. You know what I find offensive? The way people become wed to their stereotypes of anyone outside the mainstream, including sex workers and devotees of any kind. They believe the stupid clichés television feeds them."

"I agree with you. But I guess I don't see the difference between taking your views from mass-culture television and taking them from a guy with an island." I could see my candor offended her. I added, "To the extent you can sell Hover's philosophy to me, you give me ammunition. After Jim Jones, San Francisco juries are wary of devotion." These issues might never reach a jury; we both knew I was the one in need of reassurance.

"Jim Jones." She waved an exasperated hand. "And Rajneesh and

Sun Myung Moon and Maraj Ji. Yes, a lot of people set out to enlighten others and get seduced by capitalism and screwed up by power. But I'm not going to dismiss the possibility of finding a good teacher because I know there've been bad ones out there. That's stupid. I didn't drop out of law school just because I had Grosset and Philipson my first year."

I smiled. "Grosset and Philipson were certainly as bad as teachers could get. On the other hand, I can't imagine anyone drinking poisoned Kool-Aid at their request."

"Our media spotlight the negative." She shook her moussed strawberry hair. "People end up with a deep-down fear of any religion that isn't traditional. To them it sounds like paganism, devil worship; bad, go-to-hell stuff." She slapped her hand down on the desktop. "And in the process, a lot of 'sinners' become expendable. Have you noticed how often sex workers are killed in movies? Because they don't matter. They're not 'us' in the conventional sense."

I was startled by her hot-faced anger. "You heard about the women at The Back Door?"

"Yes. I didn't know the women personally—and I have mixed feelings about that club and others like it. But here's my point: I've heard dozens of conversations about the killings, and I have yet to hear one person speak those women's names. Everyone calls them the dancers or the girls or whatever. Because we're trained to consider sex workers garbage. Half the movies made in this country, prostitutes are killed just to convey a sense of danger. They're not real characters, they don't count. Only the all-American hero matters. Only Arnold Schwarzenegger."

We looked at each other a moment. I wasn't sure if an apology was in order. Because I so rarely have the impulse, I heeded it.

"I didn't mean to disparage your beliefs."

"Well." She looked down at the hand she'd slapped onto her desktop. "You can see I've taken my share of crap about them. From family especially. Friends, too. Lawyers are about as nonspiritual a group as you can find."

"There seems to be a fair number of lawyers in Brother Mike's group."

"There are probably two or three dozen of us here in the city. Reacting against the usual drill: wine tastings and the Bay Club and a bunch of cheerful bullshit instead of conversation."

"What about the other devotees? Do you know anything about the group's demographics? Professions? Income level? Age? Any of that."

She smiled wanly. "Mike's the nerd. He's probably run his mailing list through a computer-demographics program. You met Roy?"

"Yes. Look, Gretchen, you know the organization. You also know what might be legally relevant. What can you tell me? Where are the land mines?"

She leaned back in her chair, the steel suddenly out of her spine. "The video reimaging." The color bled slowly out of her cheeks. "I don't think, frankly, that Mike's heart is in the sessions anymore. Not that they aren't useful to his devotees—they truly are. And he's more than just intuitive; I believe he's a genuine avatar. But for himself . . . I think increasingly he's in it for the video manipulation. For the technology." She ran a shaky hand over her short hair.

"And it doesn't bother you, when he asks you to do those things on camera, that his motives are . . . mixed?"

"No. And I don't think it's legally relevant, either. I bring it up because I think it might be part of Arabella's claim. The important thing from my perspective—from any devotee's perspective—is that he pushes us in the direction we need to move."

"I still haven't seen the videos he made for the devotees."

Her expression brightened. "They're remarkable. For instance, there's one where a woman—Margaret, in fact—is watching Arabella elaborately seduce another woman. You see Margaret sitting there looking surfacely interested, like it's no big deal. At the same time you see two creations of Mike's, colored auras shaped like Margaret, come out of her heart. One of them's a deep, sad shade of blue. It wraps its arms around Margaret and starts consoling her—

it even gives her its thumb to suck. The other one, this big red-purple thing, flies over and tries to pull the other woman away from Arabella."

"The point being that Margaret was jealous?" It sounded pretty, but not especially insightful.

"And hurt. Babying herself on the one hand and blasting out hostility on the other." Gretchen stared through me, watching the video on an imaginary screen. "Arabella's colors flashed like a sparkler, never more than a few inches from her skin. Because for her, sensuality is in the body, in the skin. It doesn't have the cerebral and emotional content Margaret's does. The woman she was seducing, who was not a lesbian, had this little creature dancing out of her. It kept running over to the men in the group as if to say, 'Am I turning you on?'"

"That sounds a lot more interesting than what he distributed to video rental stores."

"Oh, I agree." She met my eye. "Absolutely. I think removing the animation was a mistake. But that's not what the accountants thought."

"What accountants?"

"Mike makes no secret of his reason for distributing the videos. It's a money-making endeavor. Most of his income derives from gifts and isn't taxable to him. Which means it doesn't show up on his returns, which means he has trouble establishing credit." She looked comfortable now. A lawyer discussing money. "And he has his eye on some very expensive equipment. With it, he aims to develop a level of virtual reality that incorporates holography. He's on a rampage to collect moving images to digitize. He must have talked to you about it." Her tone said, "He talks to everyone about it."

"He said something about making the imaginary real so that people begin to wonder about reality."

"Blurring the line between the so-called physical and the psychophysical, yes. It's a first step toward a new understanding of the nature of consciousness and the universe."

"And the pornography videos bring him enough money to buy the computer things he needs."

Her brows pinched into a slight frown. "The accountants did some market research—talked to the owners of The Back Door, interviewed adult-video distributors and rental-store owners. Everyone agreed: no auras. So Mike took them out. But it's important to remember he was already making the films. He didn't begin with the idea of entering the porn market. His primary motivation was to show interior aspects of our sexuality."

"But he decided to cash in on his self-awareness tool."

Gretchen's glance was sharp with irritation. "He was honest about it. His devotees understand and approve of what he's doing with the proceeds."

"When did he begin the reimaging?"

"When he arranged to market the videos. It took him and Roy and some of the other computer people months to accomplish."

"Do you think his love of technology has eclipsed his concern for devotees?" I tried to keep my tone nonjudgmental. Hadn't she, in essence, voiced that worry?

If so, she'd shored her defenses. "No, I never said that. We believe in Mike and what he's doing."

But it sounded like a question.

I considered asking her again about Margaret. I considered asking her about the women—God, it was true; I didn't remember their names—at The Back Door. But I could think of no pretext for my curiosity.

And I didn't want to push it. It might not be safe. Assuming Margaret hadn't lied, where was Gretchen when Margaret called her?

24

I STOPPED AT Margaret's apartment on my way to work. I punched her doorbell a dozen times without reply. I also stopped at Graystone Federal to open a trust account with Mike Hover's retainer. I double-checked while I was there: Margaret had indeed phoned in sick.

When I reached my office at about eleven, I had a number of telephone messages waiting. Most were from potential clients referred by other attorneys. I'd sent out engraved announcements. The expense was beginning to pay off.

I returned the calls, setting up two appointments for Monday afternoon and one for late that morning. The former involved corporate bankruptcies—the lucrative drudgery I'd left behind last year. But the latter sounded interesting. I brewed some strong coffee.

At eleven-forty, a woman introducing herself as Simone Steinem entered my office, glancing at my leased furniture with the distracted lack of interest it deserved. She was small and slender, possibly in her mid-forties, wearing a high-collared blue suit with a pastel scarf at the throat. Her brown hair was short, brushed straight back, accentuating a long neck and delicate facial structure. She carried an oversized canvas bag not nearly nice enough for her outfit.

She began by saying, "I'm told you're a kind of superlawyer. That you're very good and highly visible."

"I don't know about superlawyer. The rest is true, to some degree." She'd told me on the phone her case involved "criminal" group libel. I liked the sound of it; hoped it didn't turn out to be some kind of mild commercial slander.

"You are famous," she said. "Everyone seems to have heard of you. Would you mind if I asked you about that?"

I hesitated. Until I knew the bare bones of her problem, I risked wasting her time and mine. On the other hand, saying "No, you go first" seemed churlish. Either way, we might be wasting the morning.

"Six years ago I defended Wallace Bean." I watched for some sign she'd heard of the case. I didn't usually have to say much about Bean. Like Sirhan Sirhan and James Earl Ray, he was in the history books. "Bean shot Senators Dzhura and Hansen; you probably remember the incident."

She had a faraway look. She shook herself out of her sudden reverie. "Yes. But I'm embarrassed to say I don't remember how it worked out. Only that someone shot them; some Vietnam veteran?"

"No." I heard myself sigh. Wally Bean had fancied himself a righteous, Ramboesque pacifist; he'd equated assassinating the country's two most hawkish senators with purging our postwar demons. "Bean was insane, that's what it amounts to. That was the basis of my defense, and the jury believed that also."

"Was it you who did the television defense?"

"Bean had been inundated with television images of lone-wolf, take-the-law-in-their-own-hands good guys. But the jury didn't rely on that. They didn't use it as the basis of their verdict. They believed the psychiatric testimony that Bean was insane—independent of his television-based morality."

"But there was some flap about it, wasn't there?"

To say the least. My fall-back defense had subsequently been outlawed. "Some law-and-order politicians misstated the basis of the verdict. They used it to sell their criminal law reform package. And the press didn't distinguish between that defense and the insanity plea; they blended the two. So people believed the worst. It plugged into their preconceived notions about the system. That's politics—it had nothing to do with the jury's decision."

"It made you very famous."

She was beginning to make me nervous. I'd been badgered relentlessly after that verdict, almost exclusively by people who refused to understand the basis for it. I'd gotten a lot of hate mail, a lot of death threats; the ultra-conservative senators had been redneck icons. And Wallace Bean had been mercilessly gunned down within weeks of his release from the mental hospital.

"From my perspective as Bean's lawyer, the important thing was to do right by him." I had a catalog of bland, uninflammatory responses on the subject. I hoped she didn't make me run through more of them.

"And then you handled the Daniel Crosetti case?"

"Some years later, yes. But my primary areas of specialty are bankruptcy and corporate litigation."

"Crosetti killed an FBI agent, didn't he?"

"He never went to trial. He died first." After the government had done just about everything it could to harass and impoverish him.

"How did that case make you famous?"

I wished to God it hadn't. It had proved useless, going public to explain the government's complicity. I'd tilted at establishment windmills, and all I'd gained was the weight of Crosetti's despair. I'd spent the last ten months crawling out from under it, in fact.

"The crime got a lot of press. I was Crosetti's spokesperson, that's all." She would have to be satisfied with that.

"Well, I guess the other thing I need to ask you is if you have a case like that now. Something you'll be getting attention for."

"I don't discuss my clients' cases with other people. I'm sorry."

"But if you're going to be getting a lot of press . . . Don't you feel it's a fair question? You will be associated in the public mind with your client, won't you? You have been before."

I leaned back in my cheap cloth chair and looked at her. What the hell kind of case was she about to offer me that required me to be famous and visible, but only because of past cases.

"I'm sorry. I don't discuss my clients. There's always the possibility that one of my cases will become news. I think that's probably true of any lawyer you hire."

She slid her hand into the canvas bag on her lap. I watched, expecting her to pull out a file folder or a stack of memos. Instead she hesitated, scowling at me.

"You'll understand in a minute. It's because I know . . ." She'd grown pale. The pastel of her scarf looked almost bright against her white throat. "Isn't it true you represent a sex guru who sells films of women getting raped?"

I blinked at her. What was going on? Putting aside her crazy characterization of the case, how did she know I represented Brother Mike? There were no court filings yet. I wasn't on record anywhere as his attorney. All I'd done so far was open a trust account with his check.

"I've told you I don't discuss my clients."

"It must get addictive, defending famous criminals and being on television and giving out interviews."

"No, it doesn't. Where did you hear about—?"

"Don't you care what your client has done? Have you ever been raped yourself?"

I felt myself shut down. How many crazy people had I met since I'd taken the Bean case? They might seem normal, in their tailored suits. They might even be elected officials. But they revealed themselves in their paranoid phrases, in their refusal to see the system as an impersonal framework and not a shield against the particular evils plaguing them.

"You don't really have a case for me, do you?" A group libel case; I'd have loved that.

"I do have this for you."

She began extracting something from her bag. "From raped women," she was saying.

I'd seen the film of Senators Dzhura and Hansen a hundred times. They stood on the steps of a small chartered plane waving hello. Bean burst through the crowd like some fat, panting Bruce Willis and gunned them down.

I watched Simone Steinem's hand come out of the bag. In my mind's eye I saw Hansen stagger into Dzhura, Dzhura lurch and cling to the stair rail.

Her hand moved slowly compared to my inner newsreel. Slowly enough for me to see the senators get shot, to hear Bean cry, "For everyone who died in Vietnam."

Her hand moved slowly enough for me to hear a shout from the crowd surrounding Bean: "He's got a gun!"

I surged to my feet, the words on my tongue but not quite out of my mouth: *Got a gun!*

Her hand jerked forward, arm straightening. She definitely held something. I knocked my flimsy chair over, scurrying back, away from her, not sure what she held, only that it wasn't a file, it wasn't a memo, it was an object and it was being brandished or cast at me.

I screamed when it hit me. I watched it mark my pale jacket and shirt, I watched a dark splotch begin high and taper low. I watched it but I felt no impact, I felt no bullet; I felt nothing hit me. I watched it and tried to listen for it. Had I heard a shot? Had I heard anything except her high-pitched repetition of the phrase "From raped women?"

Still moving backward, I stumbled over the chair. I was looking down at my jacket, making small grunts of horror. It was stained red. My hands went to the stain, didn't protect me from the chair arms as I went down. They caught my back, my shoulder, my ribs.

The stain was wet. Red.

I looked up in time to see the woman run from my office. I could only see part of her, my desk was in the way. I couldn't see what was in her hand. I could only see her cap of hair and long neck.

I was rubbing at the stain, still scooting backward on the floor, still making small grunting sounds, when Pat Frankel, the lawyer across the hall, stepped in.

"My God! I did hear you scream!"

She knelt in front of me. "What happened? Are you okay?"

She stared wide-eyed at the stain. "Blood," she said.

She moved my hands aside and pulled the shirt open. Then she rocked back on her heels.

Under the stain was nothing. My skin, smeared but unbroken.

"You're not hurt." Her voice was husky with relief.

"No." Mine was, too.

She recoiled. "It looks like blood. We should majorly disinfect ourselves. Do you have any cuts on your hands or your body?" She screamed out, "Gayle! Gayle, can you hear me?"

A moment later, our secretary popped her head in.

"Oh, my God!" she said.

"She's not hurt. But we need alcohol or bleach or peroxide or something. Fast." She looked at her hands, saying, "Oh, shit. Hurry."

Gayle sputtered the beginning of a question.

"Hurry!" Pat urged.

Gayle dashed from the room.

Pat stood, helping me up. "What happened in here?"

"This woman came in." I was panting, staring at my belly, at the smooth skin; skin I'd expected to bear a wound.

"Here, you should sit." She righted my chair. "What did the woman do?"

"She asked me about being famous. About the Wallace Bean case."

Pat looked surprised. "Why?"

"I don't know. She asked me if I had any cases now that would get that kind of attention."

"Right—like you're going discuss your other clients."

"That's what I told her. Then she asked me about a case I'm working on—which I'm not on record for yet. I don't know how she knew about it. She said it involved women getting raped, and she said 'this is from raped women.' She threw this on me. I didn't know what it was. I didn't know what she was doing. If I hadn't stood up, it would have hit me in the face."

The blood of raped women. The female symbol painted on my living-room wall. I'd been targeted for representing a client viewed as anti-feminist. But Hover's philosophy seemed independent of gender. And I had nothing to do with it, anyway.

Gayle was back with a bottle of alcohol. "From the bathroom," she explained. "And paper towels." She handed me a stack.

"I'd clean that off yourself fast." Pat shuddered, pouring alcohol on towels and handing them to me. Then she poured some over her fingers where she'd touched my shirt. "And we should look around to see if she threw blood anywhere else."

"It smells." The secretary sounded surprised. "I didn't know blood smelled."

"If you've got some plastic, you should put that shirt in it and get the blood tested."

"I don't have any cuts. Even if it's AIDS-tainted, I should be okay."

"None got in your eyes, your mouth?"

I shook my head. "It would have. If I hadn't stood up."

"Then I think you should get it tested. Just so you know how crazy the person was. I really think you should. It gives it a whole different aspect, you know what I mean?"

I nodded. I represented my clients, I didn't endorse them; why couldn't people understand that?

"I've got some sweat clothes in my office. Want to borrow them? They're clean. I keep them in case I work late."

"Thanks."

The minute Gayle and Pat left, I tore my clothes off and rubbed alcohol over every millimeter of my torso. Very little blood had soaked through the fabric of my jacket and blouse. What had, I doused until no trace remained.

By the time I was done, Pat was back with her warm-up suit. She turned toward the window, giving me privacy as I changed into it.

I was calmer now. Calm enough to look around the room. Whatever container the blood had been in, the woman had taken it with her. In fact, I could see no trace of her presence, not a slip of paper or a matchbook or a gum wrapper.

She'd left only intangibles: the smell of blood, my outraged fear. And worse, the certainty that, as always, the crazies were out there, ready to misunderstand my actions and punish me for them. The world was a dangerous place, and I was alone in it.

A voice from the doorway boomed, "Laura! What the hell? What happened?"

In a second, Sandy was beside me. He stared down at my suit, in a heap on the floor. "Is that blood? What happened?"

"Someone tossed blood on me—said it was from raped women. She mentioned my case. I don't know what her story is." I could hear anger in my voice now. She'd made me afraid; damn her.

"I think I know." Pat turned away from the window, stepping toward us. "Unfortunately, I think I know who did it."

Sandy scowled at her. I just stared. In her dark suit, she made a featureless silhouette against the window.

"I'm sorry as hell," she continued. "But I bet it's my whiner. I told her you were famous. I really did a hard sell—told her what a great job you'd done for Bean, told her all about Dan Crosetti. I just wanted her off my back."

"But how would she know about my current client?"

Sandy didn't care about that. "Who is it? What did she do this for?"

"God, sometimes you just want to slap people." She stepped closer. Her tan face crinkled in apology. "Her name's Megan Carter. She's part of a group called the Women's Media Project—remember, they were at The Back Door rally. Oh no, you got there after they were kicked out. Anyway, they do lectures and slide-show presentations, with pictures out of magazines to prove the media objectifies women and puts them in subservient roles."

"That's big news." Her sweat clothes were a little tight on me, but they were preferable to the clothes I'd shucked.

"Do you remember those Minnesota women who tried to pass an anti-pornography ordinance?"

"That forbid depiction of women in postures of submission or servility?"

"Like art and literature cause the problem." A quick grin. "Anyway, that's the WMP's trip except they're not trying to pass ordinances, not since the Minnesota one got struck down. They give talks, like I said—and actually, a lot of what they say I agree with. Anyone would, it's so obvious. But they always go too far, saying they're not for censorship while they pull magazines off racks and try to shut down sex clubs. They do a lot of suffragette stuff—chain themselves to things, picket, throw the blood of raped women." She looked troubled. "But usually on sidewalks. You know, in front of beauty pageants and things. That's what her case is about—basically trespass with a First Amendment defense. But I've never known them to throw blood on *people*."

"She seemed . . ." Crazy was too strong a word, perhaps.

Pat nodded. "I know what you mean. She's out there. She's got this kind of angry-fragile thing; it's a little scary. She draws no line between pornographic images of women and women being raped. Cause and effect, and forget evidence to the contrary. Anyway, they're a sad group. Most of them have been raped; life's very painful for them. You get the feeling they'd go nuts if they couldn't do something. So they focus on pornography. Even though most of the community's accepting it. Even reclaiming it."

By "the community" I supposed she meant liberals and gay people like the ones at The Back Door rally.

"Where do they get the blood?"

"Group members donate it."

"So, literally, the blood she threw on me was from a woman who'd been raped?"

She dropped into the chair Megan Carter had vacated. "Sorry to say. And I have no idea if they screen for HIV. They're very sincere and idealistic. But they're pretty fanatic. I can find out for you."

Sandy sounded grim. "If they think magazines made someone rape them, maybe they think anyone into the status quo deserves to take their chances."

"They didn't have the opportunity to screen their rapists." Pat looked forlorn. "I'll find out. I definitely think you should get the blood tested."

Sandy was shaking his head. "This is fucked up. Throwing blood in this day and age . . ." upon a time, okay. You pour blood on draft files or wherever, you make a point. You don't put people's lives— janitors, clerks—at risk. But this is nineteen ninety-four, you know?"

I took a step away from my bloody clothes. What was it Brother Mike had said? That if they didn't find a cure for AIDS soon, the nineties would be the craziest decade ever?

"Well, one thing"—Sandy sounded calmer than he looked—"I'd say you found the person—the group, anyway—tore your place up. We better find out what else is in the works."

"I thought she was pulling out a gun." My voice was still faint with relief.

"Laura." Sandy's tone was bracing. "You need to know how fanatic they are—for your own security. Throwing your stuff around is one thing. If they're tossing unscreened blood, then they don't mind putting your life in danger."

I looked out my window. A stalled car clogged the best route to the freeway. The stench of exhaust mingled with rubbing alcohol evaporating from paper towels. I missed the smell of pine and rain.

"You okay, Laura?"

"Yes."

"I say don't take it lying down. Call the cops on them."

It took me a second to realize he meant the Women's Media Project. "They'd probably love the publicity. And they might use it as a forum to attack my client." And I was client-positive, wasn't I?

He sighed. "What's with you? You got to deal with this."

I saw six silver-taped faces staring blankly up at me. I felt scared. And guilty: I should have told the police what little I knew. I could hardly face them now with my own small problems; could hardly meet them with lies of omission.

Sandy watched me. "You been messed with too much, maybe. It's burning you out."

He pulled me into his arms. I let him think what he wanted.

25

I RETURNED TO the office after lunch and a long shower and a change of clothes. I found a telephone message waiting: *Judy Wallach called to say her client has withdrawn the claim against your client.*

My case had gone up in smoke before I'd done anything but bank the retainer.

I wondered why.

I worried that it had something to do with the attack on Arabella de Janeiro. Maybe with the murder of her coworkers.

I worried that she'd been frightened away.

I wondered what might have happened to Margaret if she hadn't decided not to sue Mike Hover.

I phoned Margaret's house. I drove there again and rang the bell several times.

Because I wasn't ready to quit. I'd seen a lot of things I could have lived my whole life without seeing. My place had been wrecked. I'd had blood thrown on me.

I couldn't just drop it.

I drove to the hospital and asked to visit Arabella de Janeiro. She'd withdrawn her claim against my client; I could speak to her without her lawyer present. I couldn't bill my client for it, but what the hell. I didn't have anything better to do, not until Monday. And my questions seemed urgent.

De Janeiro looked terrible. Her face was mottled red and purple, beginning to fade to decayed-meat green. One eye was swollen half shut. Her lips were puffy, especially on the left side. Her hair was lank and without luster, a chestnut that now looked merely brown. Her inner elbow was stuck with IV needles and bruised blue. She sipped something through a bent straw, squirming under a sheet lumpy with (I supposed) bandages.

I stepped into her line of sight and introduced myself. "I represent Mike Hover," I explained. "Do you mind if I sit down?"

She froze. Said nothing.

"I represent Mike Hover," I repeated. "I'm a lawyer."

"What are you here for? To talk about the murders?" Her eyes reddened, spilling tears. "I won't talk about it. I don't know anything. I already told the police: I don't know anything."

"I'm here to ask what happened to you."

"I don't know what happened at the club." She seemed tensed for contradiction. "I don't even know how they died. I watch the news, but they never say. Do you know?" The question was clipped, breathless.

"No." I tried to ignore the merciless image of taped faces. "You'd have been with them if you hadn't been attacked."

"Yes." The word was tight, small. "It trips me out: they did me a favor. I never would have believed it. I think about it every time it hurts."

"They?"

Her fingers jerked to her lips. "Gay hookers, I mean. The ones who slapped me around."

"Why? Why did they do that?"

"Hired."

"By who? Why?"

She stared at her drink. "You should know that."

I watched her face, wondering if I saw hostility or merely the results of her battering.

"What do you mean?"

"Well, who else could it be?" A sudden frightened glance. "What have I done different lately except make hassle for Mike Hover?"

"You're saying Hover had you beaten?"

"Well, it's kind of coincidental, don't you think? The day my lawyer talks to Roy and Rhonda, I get ambushed." Her tone was oddly petitioning. "Lucky it saved my—"

She swallowed several times.

"You know, the whole time they did this, I dreamed about getting revenge on Mike. And after, at the hospital, all I could think about was revenge. But it turned out it saved my life. Not going to work saved my life. Funny, isn't it?"

Her voice, even slurred and slowed by thick lips, had a seductive lilt. I'd clerked in a department store for a while to pay my college tuition; I remembered how the Can-I-help-you chirpiness lingered in my voice after work, maddening me.

"If Hover had this done to you, I'll withdraw as his counsel."

She shrugged. "You really think this is worse than what he did with the videos? That's pretty naive."

I hesitated. If she ever decided to reinstate her claim, her lawyer would crucify me for talking to her today.

"No," she continued. "The way it worked out . . . saving my life, I don't know. I'll probably drop it completely. Forever. You tell my sweetie I'm going to let him off the hook."

"Your sweetie."

"Didn't he tell you that? Didn't he get all poetic and transplendent about it?" A rasp afflicted her speech. She pressed her hand to her rib cage. "Son of a bitch, it hurts. Cracked rib."

"You had a relationship with Mike Hover? Besides guru-devotee?" I pulled a molded plastic chair away from the wall, closer to the bed. Behind her, a drawn blue curtain cut the room in two, separating her from another patient. It also deprived her of light from the window. But perhaps her swollen eye was photosensitive.

"Crazy in love. You know how it feels to think someone's crazy in love with you? If he's really somebody special?" She put her glass down, moving slowly. "And I'm used to gurus. I grew up in Berkeley, the original Birkenstocks-and-overalls kid. Free-thinking parents—a houseful of intense people, a lot of heavy conversation, new ideas. All that. I'm saying I'm not that easily impressed. But Mike hooked me. I used to feel like he could see right into me; like I was in this perfect telepathic universe and I could finally relax and be myself. I was flying when he fell for me—him with a jillion people looking up to him. And me your basic slut."

"Do you mind telling me about the relationship?"

Her tongue poked through her lips, moistening them but also, I thought, probing to see how swollen they were. She must not have liked what she felt. The tongue went back in quickly.

"What's it to you? No offense."

Why not? "Someone broke into my apartment and sprayed, well, trashed the place. And someone came to my office this morning claiming to have a libel case for me. It turned out she was from the Women's Media Project. She'd heard—I don't know how—that I was representing Brother Mike, and she took out a container of blood and threw it all over me. She said it was from raped women."

"Yuck." What her reaction lacked in polish it made up for in feeling.

A shudder shook my spine. "I'll be honest with you. I saw The Back Door show Tuesday night. The night after, I sat in on one of Brother Mike's sessions. And I've seen the videos."

She waited a few seconds for me to continue the thought. "I have a feeling there's a punch line."

"I don't know. This person threw raped-women's blood on me—just because I represent Hover. I don't really understand the connection."

"It's in her mind." She pushed a long lock of hair off her face. Under her bruises, she could be anyone, beautiful, ugly. But her gestures, even the simple pushing away a lock of hair, were done with practiced glamour. "I've got my problems with Mike's videos, obviously. But not with videos, period; you know what I mean? Those women are nutsoid. They don't see a bit of difference between fantasy and reality. And they don't see a bit of difference between depictions of sex and actual rape, even if the depictions are loving and consensual. They come and hassle us at the club . . ." Her face grew pinched, ashen; perhaps she realized that "the club" would be a different place now, full of strangers. "Anyway, they come on like uptight Christian ladies. It boils down to the same old bullshit: sex is dirty, men are brutes. And women are fragile little angels who need protecting from hairy beasts who—heaven forbid—look at naked bodies and come in their hands."

She sat straighter. I wondered how many times she'd made this argument; and yet, her passion seemed new. "They've figured out the world is full of victims and oppressors, and they've decided it's about sex. Like sex causes violence. They don't like clubs, they don't like porn films, they hassle the S-and-M people. Anybody who's into sex in a different way or a commercial way gets blamed for rape. It doesn't even make sense. They confront us at work maybe two, three times a year."

"Have they thrown blood?"

"Not on us, but they've thrown it in front of the theater."

"I heard they disrupted the anti-censorship rally."

"I know. And it's not fair—the couple that owns the club is very active in free speech things. They've donated a lot of money to good causes—not necessarily related to sex. And one of the reasons they can afford to pay us more lately is they're not spending half their income on lawyers to keep the theater open. They're good employers. I mean, what the anti-sex women don't get is that we sell our time, just like anybody else. Yes, we fuck our work buddies, and

we do it in public. We like that; we wouldn't be in the industry if
we didn't like to fuck in public. There's nothing wrong with that.
No one's coercing us. And the men who come to our shows really
appreciate what we do. They're grateful. They need to see women
who love sex—you know, maybe the women in their lives don't.
They need to see women who aren't hung up, who like to show
themselves off and touch themselves and be touched. There's nothing bad about that. We like it. They like it. Isn't that what work's
supposed to be?"

For a little more inspiration, I'll put it in deeper. "You must have
nights when you're not in the mood."

"Any job's a job sometimes."

"When I was there, I noticed one of the dancers had bruises all
over her thighs."

"Yeah, well. And boyfriends are boyfriends. What can I tell you?
Some of my coworkers are smart, and some aren't. Some are bitches."
Her face clouded. "Were."

"Why were you going to sue Brother Mike?" It was an unprofessional question. If she ever resurrected her claim, I'd have to answer
to the court for it. It surprised me that I needed a response more
than I needed to hedge my bets.

"He was using me." Her throaty voice dropped in pitch. "Son of
a bitch."

"What do you mean?"

"He wanted me in the videos because my body's good and I know
a lot of tricks. And I got the groups charged up—sometimes I'd do
my act before the sessions to get people going; I'd do some sucking
to get them jacked. That was okay because that's what I do and I
like it and we agreed on it. But that wasn't enough for him. He
crossed my line. He pimped me out."

I was out of my depth. If the things she'd described were fine,
what wasn't?

"It turned out all he wanted was frames—frames of video to play
with. I could have been anyone. I gave him my love and I gave him

my body to kind of spread around. And that didn't mean a thing to him. He just wanted some celluloid. To mess with. And I was in love with him. I admired his brains and his soul and all that. I'd have done anything for him." Tears spilled from the corners of her eyes. "I did a lot of things for him that were really special, that he couldn't have gotten from anyone else in his group. And when it came right down to it, he didn't care. I could have been anybody."

"But the things you did, they weren't any different from what you do at The Back Door." Not a question.

"But that's my career. No one's using me."

"What made you go see a lawyer?"

"He'd been making all these tapes of me. He'd set the camera up and paint dots on me and have me do things. His computer would connect the dots so he'd have this like wire puppet on the screen. He'd wrap textures over it and move it around. Or he'd do stuff with lasers—set up mirrors and steel boxes, he said for making holograms. Or he'd put on the video of a session and tape me imitating one of the women. Sometimes he'd film us fucking. He'd fuck me awhile, then get up and fiddle with the machines and then come back and fuck me some more. He could keep a hard-on all day, it seemed like. I used to kid him it was the computers that turned him on, not me."

"What was he trying to do?"

"I'm not totally sure. He was into morphing—you know what that is? He'd take some dumpy devotee's body and make it like sixty percent my body—better than airbrushing, I'll tell ya. He used my friends' . . . some other people's bodies, too, getting the videos ready for rental stores. What he did with the other stuff, the holograms and line puppets and all that, I don't know."

"So why did you leave the group?"

She looked at her hands, resting on the sheet over her belly. "I may not be the swiftest, but I finally got it that it wasn't a joke. His hard-on really was for the computers and the video gadgets. I finally got it he was just using me to improve the movies. He morphed me with Rhonda—that fat cow." Again, tears spilled from her eyes. "And I'm not just anybody. I'm not just a body. I'm the one who got everyone excited. I'm the one who taught him standard setups and camera angles and all that. Ironic, huh? Because that's all he cared about, not me, not any human. Just the machines, just the equipment. The future, as he calls it."

I thought back on my day with him. He'd seemed willing to address his devotees' concerns and needs, perhaps; but I'd seen no sign that he cared for them.

"I mean, I still think he's a great man." Her voice was smaller now. "He can look right into people and see what's in there. But he doesn't really give a shit." She sat up slightly. "He's like the kind of friend who can always figure out what's wrong with your TV or your dishwasher, and so every time he goes anywhere he ends up fixing all the broken appliances for everyone. But that's just because he can. And there's no reason not to do what you can, especially if it makes people happy and makes them love you and give you money. Like that rich guy who gave him the island—he ended up going bankrupt after that. I mean, if you can tune into people on a deep level, you can end up with a group that'll do what you want. You can just play with them. Use them to work on your projects, you know?"

"You think—"

"And I won't be used! I won't. Not by anyone. That's why I'm a dancer. It gives me the control. Me."

There was a load of personal history in that "me." Clearly someone had controlled her to an intolerable level at some point in her life.

"So you were going to allege that Brother Mike tricked you into thinking he was helping you when all he was doing was using you."

"Vitiating my consent. That's what my lawyer said."

It pained me. The lawsuit would have been bigger and more complicated than anything Judy Wallach had hinted at. (Smart of her to pull her punches.) It would have been fascinating.

"Why did you change your mind about the suit?"

She pointed to her face.

I waited. "You're saying the beating happened because you went to a lawyer?" Roy and Rhonda had visited Judy Wallach that day. When I spoke to Hover the next afternoon, he told me they'd just returned with a letter from her. That meant they'd spent the night. They'd had the time—and motive—to arrange de Janeiro's beating.

"You tell me what else I've done lately that I haven't been doing for a long time." Her voice quavered. "The lawyer's the only thing, right?"

Roy and Rhonda were back on the mainland. Where was Margaret? Was she safe from them?

"Have you heard from Margaret Lenin? Have you seen her? She sounded . . . very upset last time I spoke to her. The night you were attacked."

De Janeiro didn't look surprised. "Margaret gets like that sometimes when she drinks. She told me she called someone—you, I guess. She rambles about her mother. She gets over it. She sneaked in here later and spent the night on a chair. She's okay."

"So she came back here that night?"

"Yeah. For a scene I didn't need. I can't fucking win with Margaret. I mean, if I don't call her, she gets huffed out. If I do call her, it's recriminations up the wazoo."

"But she's all right."

"More than all right." Bitterness energized her voice. "She likes me in one place, she likes me staying put. She sneaked in again yesterday and spent the night. They were going to let me go home, but my doc didn't come sign the papers like he was supposed to, so I had to stay. I'm still waiting for him. But at least they aren't dicking with me every hour like they were."

I had to ask again. "Margaret came here after she phoned me? She's really okay?"

This time Arabella sounded angry. "Why wouldn't she be? Those women were my friends, my buddies. She didn't much like them. Or you could say, the idea of them."

She waved me away, rolling onto her side. "They were nice kids, most of them. At heart, you know?"

I stared at her back, shaking with sobs. I stared at the smooth skin where the hospital gown gapped.

I didn't know what to make of her.

I HADN'T BEEN to Sandy's office in over a year. His secretary didn't seem to recognize me. She flashed me an unfriendly look and told me he was with a client.

I told her I'd wait, and I sat on a vinyl banquette that might have come from a dentist's office. The secretary (Jean? Janet?) occasionally cast me a hostile glance. I had a sudden intuition that she did remember me; that her hostility was unrelated to my having no appointment. I regarded her with more interest: mid-twenties, fluffy hair, too much makeup, too-tight clothes on a good, if hippy figure. She and Sandy were romantic, or at least sexual; I could feel it in her angry appraisal of me. I wanted to reassure her: if things went well, if I could pull the chestnuts out of the fire, Sandy and I would get back to being friends. Good friends, old friends. I'd missed him.

It was funny, though—after the shit Sandy'd given me for tumbling into McGuin's arms; calling him a "goddamn kid," if I remembered correctly. This woman couldn't be much more than half Sandy's age.

Sandy's office door opened, and I rose, expecting him to emerge. But it wasn't Sandy who came bolting out. It was Steve Sayres.

Sayres nearly plowed into me. When he saw me, he stopped as abruptly as if he'd hit a wall.

He waved an exasperated arm, as if my presence proved his angriest contention.

I was startled. Steve took his employer status seriously; he took everything about himself seriously. Sandy was a mere hireling. Why had Steve come here rather than summon Sandy?

Steve looked elegantly casual in a lightweight blue blazer and gray slacks, no tie at the neck of his white shirt. I noticed a United Airlines ticket folder in his breast pocket. Instead of a briefcase, he carried a black leather overnight bag.

His just-right tan suffused with color, making him look a little drunk. "I might have known," he said through tight lips. "They have a word for this."

Before he could tell me what the word was, Sandy stood behind him. "You're wrong, Steve. And if you don't hurry, you're going to miss your plane." His voice had a cop's authority.

Steve pivoted so we'd both be in his field of vision. "This is outrageous." Then, as if it were much worse: "This is unprofessional."

"Now hold on." Sandy stood a little too still. "You know I've got other clients."

"That's different than working both sides of the fence."

"What fence?" I'd been wondering how to make sense of Steve's presence. I could only assume Sandy had refused, perhaps repeatedly refused, a summons. Why would he do that? Why would he make Steve come here? Unless Steve was right. Unless Sandy had a conflict.

Could it be Michael Hover? Sandy had mentioned investigating Brother Mike as part of another case. Perhaps the case was Steve's. Most of Sandy's work came from White, Sayres.

I turned to Sandy, broadcasting a nonverbal demand: Explain Steve's anger.

Instead Sandy said, "Two separate matters for two separate clients. I already told you I can't say more than that. But you've got no cause for concern, Sayres."

"Then why the cat-and-mouse bullshit—why didn't you return my calls?" Sayres face was pinched.

"We just got through discussing that." Sandy's eyelids drooped. He leaned against the secretary's desk. She gazed up at him as if at Michelangelo's *David*.

"No, we bloody didn't," Steve disagreed. "You told me to lump it."

"You know I didn't say that." A smile twitched across Sandy's lips. "You got your report. You've got no call—"

"Spare me." Steve faced me. "How long have you represented Michael Hover?"

How had he learned that? Not from Sandy, I was sure.

I reviewed my transactions on Hover's behalf: I'd flown to his island, but how would Sayres know that? I'd spoken to Arabella de Janeiro's lawyer, but why would she pass the information on? And I'd deposited his retainer check in a trust account.

At Graystone Federal. Sayres's client.

"I do represent him. Obviously not long, since I've only been in business five days." One of Graystone's VPs must have phoned Sayres with the news. "Why did Graystone call you?"

He frowned, taking a small backward step. Client-account information is supposed to be confidential. The VP should have kept his mouth shut.

"They're not usually so loose-lipped," I observed.

"I didn't say anything about Graystone." But Steve's accusatory glance at Sandy made it clear he thought Sandy had.

"You don't know why Michael Hover asked me to represent him. You don't know that it has anything to do with Graystone. So I suggest you accept Sandy's assurance there's no conflict of interest on his part."

In fact, Sandy wouldn't be working with me if there were. That meant Graystone's problem with Brother Mike was unrelated to the sex videos. It must have something to do with a bank account or a loan.

I felt an ironic sympathy for Steve. He'd assumed I was out of his face as well as out of his office. And all of a sudden, here I was. Apparently with the collusion of "his" detective.

"You're going to miss that plane," Sandy repeated.

Steve did something I'd only seen him do a few times. He exploded. "Fuck you, Arkelett! You're off this case. And if I can pull you off the rest of our cases without damage to the clients, I'll do that, too."

"Don't be hasty, Steve. This lady"—Sandy nodded toward me—"punches your buttons, that's all. I've been doing right by you and right by your clients for what, seven years? Eight years?"

I looked at Sandy, tall against the backdrop of his admiring secretary. Sayres wouldn't stop being an asshole just because he'd been called on it; Sandy must know that.

Sayres pushed past, shoving me with unthinking anger. I slapped his arm away. He wasn't going to bulldoze me without consequences. Not again.

"You're off this case," he repeated.

"Far as I'm concerned," Sandy told his rushing back, "this tantrum didn't happen, Steve; remember that. I'm off this one anyway—I already turned in my report. But just for the record, I didn't hear the other stuff you said. You chill out and think better of it, don't even give it a thought; it didn't happen."

Sayres paused at the door, shoulders hunched. If his impulse was to wheel around and tell Sandy off, sever the professional relationship, he mastered it.

He walked out the door. I guess he knew Sandy was right. There was no reason to upset a long, mutually profitable association. Sayres was just being cranky. He'd get over it.

I tapped Sandy's arm. "I'd have told the obnoxious ass to go screw himself."

Sandy grinned. "He's not so bad."

"How can you say that?"

"The man gives me inspiration."

The secretary looked bewildered when I burst out laughing. She looked irritated when Sandy joined me. A private joke: she'd have a hard time if she couldn't accept the fact that we shared a lot of them, Sandy and I.

I turned to her. "I think we met before I left town last year. I'm Laura Di Palma." It would be easier being friends with Sandy if his girlfriend didn't hate the idea. "Your name's Jan, if I remember right."

"Janette." Her makeup looked almost neon around the eyes and at the lips, but she was pretty. She was feminine-looking; that would suit a traditional ex-cop like Sandy.

"Another time when I don't have to talk business with Sandy, I hope you'll let me buy you both a drink."

"Sure." She looked less than thrilled with the idea. She cast a "What gives?" glance at Sandy.

"You offering to buy me a drink right now?" he asked.

"Yes. I just came from the hospital."

He raised his brows. "Let's go."

He walked me to the door, then turned back and muttered a few words to Janette.

As we stood waiting for the elevator, he was grinning.

Finally I asked, "What's so funny?"

He held the elevator door open while I preceded him in. "You offering to buy me and Janette a drink."

"So?"

"Darn nice of you." The door closed and he hit the lobby button. "But she's not my girlfriend."

"Oh."

"Want to know what else is funny?"

"What?"

"She doesn't act like she is."

"Yes, she does. She *gazes* at you."

He shook his head. "She *gazes* at twentysomething studs with big muscles and weird hair."

We rode the fifteen floors in silence.

Before the doors reopened, he added, "So quit being gracious. You ain't gettin' off that easy."

27

WE WERE IN Sandy's car; a new Mazda, sporty but not the kind that looks like a hockey puck. It was sleek without calling attention to itself; he could park in most neighborhoods. He was smart about those things; I liked that. He shifted gears smoothly and didn't slide backward on hills. Trivial stuff, but it pleased me.

We zipped past the clock tower of the Ferry Building. I assumed he was taking me to the Marina, where there were plenty of bars, even some nice quiet ones tourists had yet to discover.

I settled into the bucket seat and enjoyed the ride. Twilight in San Francisco has it all: golden light skating over the bay and flashing off glass, the flicker of street lamps, the menthol rush of eucalyptus in the wind, fog combing treetops. The lawns of Marina Park were a brilliant emerald, dotted with people loitering, loosening their ties, pulling rainbow caps over dreadlocks, jogging behind three-wheel strollers. I considered Steve Sayres's anger.

"You want to know what I think, Sandy?"

"Depends."

"On?"

"If it has to do with my earlier investigation of your client." He glanced at me. "Because I can't talk about that."

"Then listen." I wouldn't have asked for confirmation regardless. "Margaret told me she got involved with Brother Mike because one of her debtors was involved with him. That means one of Graystone's debtors. And, as you know, Graystone Federal is Steve's client."

He took a sharp left onto Steiner, past embellished stucco houses set like jewels into tiny landscaped grounds. He didn't comment.

"So Graystone is having problems with its debtor. And, what, the debtor's giving assets away to Brother Mike? The same old triangle—creditor, debtor, recreational other?"

Sandy drove on.

"Deadbeat client gives away assets Graystone wants to go after—an island, for instance." I paused. "And Sayres steps in to try to get the asset back. He hires you to investigate—to find a way to void the gift to Hover. I heard the man who gave away the island went bankrupt afterward. I'll bet we have a match."

"So . . . you say talked to Arabella today?"

"Go ahead, change the subject." I was sure I was right. "Yes, I did talk to Arabella. She's in some pain, but she seems okay. She's furious with Mike Hover for exploiting her. She says all he cares about is having his own film to manipulate—no copyright problems. She thinks he used her to get the group hot so he could film it—"

"And play with the film? Sounds pretty cold. Is that your impression of him?"

I'd been pondering that. "Actually, yes. He's got a way of engaging your attention and focusing on who he thinks you are—I can see why people find that seductive. But there's something distracted about it. He compares what he does with his devotees to water witching. He views it as an unconscious thing he's able to accomplish."

"So Mike Hover can do this thing, this spiritual trick, and it gets him devotees. But you don't think he's into having devotees for its own sake. Or for their sake?"

"Maybe. To be fair, I only spent a day with him." And I'd found his "witching" of me infuriating. "But I didn't see him come alive until he put his hands on a computer. Even if he didn't start out making the videos just for the footage, once he began reimaging them, maybe that became the payoff."

"And that makes Arabella feel used? Same lady works at The Back Door?"

"Yes. She distinguishes between what she does for a living and what she does for love."

Sandy nodded. "Well, I'm with her on that one. She say anything about the murders?"

"No. She asked me if I knew how the women"—God, I had to learn their names; Gretchen was right, they were individuals—"were killed. The way she asked me: it was so urgent. Fearful, even. It must be terrible, knowing she'd have been with them. Why don't the police give her some information? Maybe it would trigger a recollection."

"Assuming she didn't get herself beat up as an alibi." A sidelong glance. "If Homicide thought she was being straight, they wouldn't hold back. I think they're hoping she'll trip up, say something she shouldn't know."

I replayed a mental tape of our conversation. "She didn't with me. And she does have a hell of an alibi: she got admitted to the hospital before the murders."

He slowed the car. "Number one, they're not sure exactly when the murders happened. If it was right after the ticket guy left, she might have had time. Either way, she could have hired someone. I think the cops are smart to play it this way."

Sandy parked the car in front of a relatively modest house. I assumed we were as close to the bar of his choice as he thought we were likely to get. Parking in the Marina always means a bit of a hike.

I reached for my door handle. A Stoli would be the smoothest thing in the world right now.

He turned to me, making no motion to get out of the car. "Laura?"

I stopped. His voice had a hear-me-out quality.

"This is Megan Carter's place." He pointed behind him at a two-story stucco with four mailboxes beside the door.

"The woman who threw the blood on me."

"Yuh. And maybe trashed your place."

"I was beginning to taste my drink. You know that?"

"Next stop, the Balboa. I promise."

"What's it going to accomplish, knocking at her door?" I hoped he wasn't going to lay any man's-gotta-do-what-a-man's-gotta-do bullshit on me. "We're not going to change her politics—you know that. And I'm tired. I'm pissed at her. I've got nothing to say to her except 'Fuck you.'" And I want that Stoli.

"You see her now and you'll know one way or the other whether you need to worry about her—for all you know, pouring blood on you is her new mission in life. Also find out if the blood was screened for AIDS. Plus, I'm along in case she gets weird."

I sighed. "I was hoping you'd give me some macho reason, so I could contemptuously dismiss it."

The front door was behind an ornate grille. We pressed a button labeled "No. 4 Carter." My hope of imminent relaxation fled when an intercom speaker rasped, "Who is it, please?"

Sandy gestured to me.

"Laura Di Palma." I almost added, Fuck you. "I want to talk to you about whether the blood you threw was HIV-screened."

Sandy nodded his approval. Easy enough for people to stay behind locked doors if they thought you were irrationally upset.

Still, it must have been a full minute before she said, "All right."

When a buzz indicated the door had been unlocked, Sandy pushed it open. In addition to the electronically locked grille and front door, stickers on barred windows in the entryway proclaimed the house to be silent-alarm wired. Since the downstairs doors were labeled 1 and 2, we climbed to the next flight. Megan Carter stood inside her partially open door, her face as grim and hopeless as a prisoner's.

She was obviously displeased to see I had a companion. But she stood aside and let us enter her apartment.

It was a studio, painted pale lemon, its wood floors waxed and its windows draped with yellow-and-blue-striped curtains. The kitchen-area counters were tiled blue. Megan Carter's landlord obviously had taste—and charged enough rent to exercise it.

By contrast, Carter's furniture was cheap and sparse, with fruit-crate end tables, flimsy directors' chairs and a futon on an unvarnished frame. There was nothing on the walls, not a photograph or a print or a mirror. Most women in their forties had amassed more goods. I wondered if she'd left her household treasures elsewhere, maybe left a domestic partner with them.

Her posture was of rigid challenge. "How did you find me? Did Pat tell you who I was?"

In a T-shirt and leggings she looked fragilely thin. Her face was pale and drawn. She kept her distance from Sandy.

"My friend"—I nodded toward him—"is a private investigator."

She seemed to shrink into herself when she addressed him. "How did you find me?"

"Only one group in town throws blood of raped women. Pretty simple from there." His tone was cool but not hostile; not what it might have been if she hadn't looked afraid of him.

"What do you want?" She addressed me now. "You've seen his videos—you know he promotes violence against women." A husky tremolo seized her voice. "We don't advocate censorship—that's a media lie. We ask people to speak out in some way, in whatever way they're comfortable. Many of us choose civil disobedience."

"What you did wasn't civil disobedience. It was assault. You scared the hell out of me."

"Now you know how it feels."

"How what feels? Rape? You don't know anything about me. You don't know whether I've been raped. You don't know anything about my motives for handling this case."

Her lips pinched and her nostrils flared. "You're the one who doesn't know anything: You don't know what it's like to grow up abused and get into the pornography industry because it's more of the same. Or what it's like to live in the street. Or what it's like to finally get a break and get a job that lets you feel decent. To start a relationship and a family, and then have all that—everything you've worked for and care about—go up in smoke."

"I didn't cause your problems."

"Can you say the same about Michael Hover?"

"Yes."

"People always assume we're coming from a position of innocence. They assume we're trying to protect our own little puritan sweetness. But we're not; we come from a position of experience, of inside knowledge." She turned, paced the few steps into her kitchen area, then turned and paced back. "I'm a good person. I raised two boys—it's not that I hate men, believe me; I always enjoyed my boys and their friends." Gloom settled over her features. "Oh, I'd hear the remarks they made; I was aware of the damage being done to them. The way they talked about women—exactly the way television presents them, as T and A. I sat down to watch football with them one afternoon and I got so discouraged. These were nice boys raised by smart women, and still they were brainwashed. That's how powerful media images are. It reminded me of when I was in high school, going to James Bond movies with my dates and walking out afterward so depressed. All these impossibly beautiful women with nothing on their minds but lust. Having to act like that to be popular. Having to act like Pussy Galore. And what did I get for it?"

Sandy and I exchanged glances.

"I am a good person." She blinked rapidly, focusing on me. "I hear what you're saying about the blood—and it's not easy for me to do things like that. But someone's got to shock people out of their complicity. If I shocked you into understanding who your client is . . ."

"I have my own perceptions about who he is. And you can't assault me into changing my mind."

She looked a little rattled. "You're talking like a lawyer arguing a case. I'm talking about the reality of what happens to women because of Brother Mike. Can't you see that?"

"People make their own choices. It's maternalistic of you to try to force your—"

"Choice! They don't have a choice—they've given that power away to him! Don't you see? He wins their devotion and then persuades them into sexual behavior that's alien to them, repugnant to them." Her eyes grew bright with tears. "Haven't you seen the videos? People are being obviously raped." I wondered if she meant Gretchen. "For his profit. How can you defend that?"

"I may have problems with the basis of their consent. But they did consent."

She took a disconcerted step backward. "So you'll just sit by— no, worse than that—use your advocacy skills to defend violence against women?" Her tone was of genuine wonderment.

I glanced at Sandy. The meeting was going exactly as I'd have predicted. But he was right. Megan Carter was no longer a scary unknown; I no longer feared her.

Sandy spoke. "Was the blood HIV-screened?"

"It's my blood," she informed us. Standing there, pale arms wrapped around herself, she didn't look as if she had any to spare. "I'm HIV-negative. They tested me after I got"—a few deep breaths— "attacked. I didn't know if I wanted them to. I had to wait six months, and the whole time I felt I'd go insane if they tested me and I came out positive. I wondered how I'd feel about cradling my grandchildren—did I really believe it wasn't transmittable? My partner wouldn't get into the hot tub with me, and I didn't blame him, really. But it did surprise me that after so many years together, all it took was a few months of depression to kill our relationship."

"You were going to put me through that." I couldn't keep the bitter anger out of my voice. "If I hadn't stood up, if it had hit me in the face, if I hadn't had a private detective to track you down—" I wanted to hit her. "Six months to find out it wasn't tainted blood."

"Did you see anybody using condoms on those videos?" she countered. "Those women could be getting infected as well as raped."

"And that gives you the right to spread the worry to me?" I finally said what I'd come to say: "Fuck you."

"I'm a good person," she repeated. "I'm a soldier. You have to be, to do any good in the world."

"Sandy, goddamn it." You got me into this.

"Did you break into Laura's apartment?"

Carter scowled at the pristine oak floor.

Sandy took a menacing stride toward her. "Did you break in—"

"Perhaps someone else in the group," she said tersely. "We're foot soldiers, not privy to the full strategy."

Who was their general? I wondered.

"We exist to make a point," she continued. "We don't harm people."

"Bullshit!" Sandy's voice was sour with contempt. "You throw blood on them."

"We wanted to make her think. Just like we made Michael Hover . . ."

"Made Michael Hover think? How? What are you talking about?" I took a step closer. "Did one of your people handcuff him?"

She crimped her lips as a child would: *You can't make me tell*.

"You sent somebody to the island to pose as a devotee, is that right? That's how you found out I represent Hover. One of your people either saw me or heard about me there."

Again no answer. But her eyes gleamed a triumphant, *yes*!

"What would you have done to him if he hadn't called out? If there hadn't been someone in the hall to respond?"

"We don't harm people," she repeated.

"You were just going to leave him handcuffed?"

She said nothing. If the object had been to render him powerless, his "humiliation" had been brief. After running into me, Rhonda had gone upstairs and found him, unlocking him with a handcuff key of her own.

"Unlike *him*"—her hatred italicized the word—"we don't engage in violence."

"I need that drink, Sandy."

He opened the front door, motioning me out with a jerk of the head.

As I stepped through, I had a sudden curiosity about the case Megan Carter had been urging Pat to take. But I was almost out of the mire now. I felt too tired and sullied to want to jump back in.

Out in the car, Sandy apologized. "I know it was a drag. But at least you know what her trip is. Now she's said her piece, maybe they won't hassle you again. Right?" He looked guilty, in need of my reassurance.

"I understand why you took me there. And yes, I feel comfortable about going back home now, which is good. But I'm not in a grateful mood, Sandy. Let me be pissed off awhile longer."

"I had another reason for wanting to talk to Carter. I think the Women's Media Project taped the women, Laura. I think they went to The Back Door to lecture them, give them that slide show your lawyer friend described. Force them to sit through it."

"You think the Media Project killed them?" They seemed more prone to make a "statement" and run. As angry as I was, I couldn't see Carter committing murder. Or maybe that would undermine my newly regained feeling of security. Maybe I didn't want to believe it.

"That's what bothers me. Taping the women to face the stage: to me, that sounds like Carter and her group. Taping up the faces, no. No. I can't see them doing that. So either it's a coincidence this group's on the warpath, or someone found those women taped and went for it. Killed them for reasons of their own."

Margaret? Had Margaret found the women bound to their seats? Had she taped the faces of her "rivals"?

Sandy stopped at a light. He watched me. "What do you know that I don't, Laura?"

If it happened that way, I'd withheld key information from the police. I could be viewed as an accessory after the fact.

There was only one way to make sure Sandy couldn't be accused of the same: "Nothing."

He shook his head. When the light changed, he laid scratch getting me to a bar.

I WENT BACK to my apartment that night. I had enough Stoli in me to ignore the mess. I'd deal with it in the morning. Sandy was right: Confronting Megan Carter had given my fear context. Carter had done me very little harm. Especially compared to the injury she nursed.

And the discharge of tension was enough to sink me into deep sleep, my first in days.

I was in the shower the next morning when Mike Hover called.

I stood wrapped in towels, listening to his message on my machine. It began with a pause.

"Um . . . I heard you're looking for me, but I don't know what— Do you need to talk? I'll wait to hear from you. I've been distressed about those murders. I used every one of the women in my videos, did you know that? For morphing purposes. I keep feeling I'm responsible in some way; I don't know how, but it's a strong feeling, stronger since I've been back down here. I'd be interested in your opinion as a lawyer. Is it the kind of intuition one takes to the police? I'll wait to hear from you."

Back down here. Of course he'd keep a place in San Francisco; very likely a gift from a follower. Most of his devotees were still here. Maybe more important, cutting-edge computer products were developed and available here. Silicon Valley was probably his Mecca.

So why didn't I have his local address? Why hadn't Roy and Rhonda supplied it? I seemed to remember asking for it. They must have known I'd need it.

Six dancers and a boyfriend had been killed. Margaret had been calling in sick and not answering her phone or doorbell. Brother Mike was back.

I sat down with a cup of coffee. I felt stupid; things weren't falling into place.

I didn't know Brother Mike's local address. Why not?

Because Roy and Rhonda hadn't given me one. Because Brother Mike didn't have a place here. Not a place of his own.

That meant when he stayed here, he stayed with someone.

It wouldn't be Arabella. Until yesterday, she'd planned to sue him. Even if he'd once thought of her place as "his," subsequent events would have changed his view.

It wouldn't be Margaret. She too had contemplated suing him. And she might be jealous of him, not likely to be hospitable now.

Gretchen, on the other hand, had demonstrated a willingness to take care of Brother Mike. She'd talked Margaret out of suing him. She'd arranged for me to be his lawyer.

I phoned her office first. The receptionist snapped that Gretchen wasn't in. Her exasperation might have been a by-product of working on Saturday. Either that or Gretchen had received an unusual number of calls that morning.

I tried Information next. They listed neither a home phone number nor an address. *The Parker Directory of California Attorneys* predictably showed only a business listing. But I riffled its pages until I found the names of two of our law-school classmates. One was in her office that morning.

She was surprised to hear from me. She was even more surprised by my request. She didn't have Gretchen's address and number in her Rolodex, she told me. But she gave me the name of someone who did.

Within ten minutes, I had the information I wanted.

I left Sandy a message bringing him up-to-date.

I tried repeatedly to reach Gretchen. In the meantime, I reordered my living room. It was less of a chore than I'd imagined.

By the time I was done cleaning, I'd given up on telephoning.

29

LIKE MARGARET, Gretchen lived in my old neighborhood. I stood before her small-from-the-outside, shared-wall stone house. On either side were miniature Queen Annes. The street was lined with broad-leafed trees. The air was fresh with menthol from the Presidio's eucalyptuses.

I rang her bell, noticing it was the only one on the panel: a real house, not an apartment. But then, she'd made partner. I'd have invested in a house if I'd made partner. Maybe that would have made working with Steve Sayres bearable.

When I didn't get an answer, I rang again, clinging to the possibility that she was home and Brother Mike was with her.

I put my finger on the buzzer and I kept it there. I'd been through too much to be ignored. Whatever the basis for Mike's "feeling," I had a right to hear it.

My persistence finally paid off. I saw an upstairs curtain shift slightly. Someone had been there watching. A few moments later, the door opened, just a crack.

Gretchen, widening the gap a few more inches, looked pale and tense. She wore a green jersey outfit that might have been pajamas or might have been a warm-up suit. She was barefoot, and her strawberry hair lacked its moussed discipline. It fell over her forehead like a Beatle cut.

She stared at me. That's all. She didn't say anything.

"Brother Mike's here, isn't he?"

"He was," she admitted. "He went out early this morning, and he's not back yet." Her eyelids opened wider, then wider still, as if to telegraph some thought to me.

"He left me a message, Gretchen. I'd like to talk to him, find out what he meant."

"I'll tell him to call you."

"He's been here a day or two?"

"Since yesterday." She cast a nervous glance over her shoulder.

"Do you mind if I come in?" Maybe he'd discussed his "feeling" with Gretchen.

She shook her head slightly, again glancing back without turning her head. "I can't talk now."

Someone was there with her.

"Are you—" I stopped. Why ask if she was in trouble? Why ask if someone was there with her? She would say no, either way.

"I could come back, Gretchen." I put my hand on the doorknob. I opened my eyes unnaturally wide, as she had done.

She looked at my hand on the knob. "Yes." After a pause: "Because this isn't a good time."

"Okay." I turned and walked away. I didn't hear the door close until I was at the bottom of the steps. I walked on down the block and around the corner.

I stood there awhile. My impression was that I'd made a deal with Gretchen to return and let myself in. I reviewed the conversation; was that what Gretchen had intended?

And if so, was it a good idea?

Earlier in the week, I'd almost walked into a bullet. I'd walked into a theater full of dead women. I needed to be more careful.

I looked up the leafy residential block, trying to get my bearings. It was my old stamping ground; where was the nearest telephone?

I began walking toward the Presidio. The big house servicing the golf course would surely have a phone.

I hurried. The three-block walk took me by my old apartment. I noticed wooden blinds in the windows. I wondered what else the new tenant had done with the place. I supposed she had more time to decorate than I'd had.

I passed the stone fence leading into the Presidio. Irresolute fog meandered over the greens. Carts with bright surreys faded into it.

The clubhouse entrance was blocked by handsome seniors in Izod shirts and plaid pants. A polite "Excuse me" got me past them.

I found a phone in the airy lounge. I reached Sandy's answering machine. I knew he'd check his messages frequently. He'd be expecting to hear from me again.

"Hi, Sandy. If you've been checking your machine, you know I planned to go to Gretchen Miller's house. Well, she acted strange when she answered her door. I think she's in trouble. I think she left her door unlocked, expecting me to let myself in. I'm going back to do that. You've got her address from my last message. I'll meet you there, or I'll call you again."

I hung up. Should I do more? Should I call the police?

I stood with the receiver in my hand, replaying my conversation with Gretchen. I wasn't sure. She might be ill, she might be feeling antisocial. She hadn't actually asked for help. I might be wrong.

I didn't have cause to call the police. But I wanted someone other than Sandy to know where I was. Sandy might not get the message.

I phoned Hyerdahl's office. Pat Frankel answered.

"Pat, hi. This is Laura Di Palma. This is going to sound a little weird."

"Good! If I have to work on the weekend, I at least want some spicy—"

"I've been trying to get through to Sandy—remember him?—my detective. But I haven't been able to. Could you"—how could I avoid sounding paranoid?—"could you do me a favor and jot down an address? It's where I'll be. I need him to meet me there. If he comes by my office, maybe you could give it to him."

"All right." She sounded surprised.

I recited Gretchen's address. I wondered how much more I should say.

"Um . . . Laura, are you okay and all that? I mean, I've been worried about you. Is this Megan Carter's address?"

"No. It's Gretchen Miller's."

"Do I know Gretchen Miller?"

"I don't know."

"The name's familiar. I know I've heard it."

"She works for Millet, Wray and Weissel."

"Oh, wow. She's the one who did the porn film."

I was stunned. "How did you know about that?"

"Oh, God. It's major gossip. Millet, Wray found out yesterday. They're having kittens over there. Stodgy old firm like that. I give her points, I really do. I was even thinking of renting—"

I hung up. I felt relieved, even a little silly. No wonder Gretchen was behaving oddly, not answering her phone. She was hiding out; avoiding gossip and employer anger. She'd played chicken with her career and she'd lost (or won, if Brother Mike was correct). I wondered if her golden parachute would be as substantial as mine had been. I wondered if the senior partner of Millet, Wray wanted her out as much as Doron White (influenced by Steve Sayres) had wanted me out.

Well, I hoped she'd be wiser with her severance pay than I'd been with mine. I hoped she'd take care of herself instead of some boyfriend. Instead of some guru.

I walked back to her house. The more I thought about it, the more certain I became that Gretchen's behavior had been sincerely antisocial; that our "bargain" had been projection on my part; that she simply wished to be left alone until her mood improved.

At her door, I hesitated. If it was unlocked, if I went ahead inside, how would I explain my presence?

I turned the handle. If I had incorrectly interpreted our conversation, I would be honest about it. And I'd ask her a few questions about Brother Mike.

I pushed the door gently. It opened a crack. I positioned myself so that I could see into the wainscoted entry. I opened the door a little farther. I could see into adjoining rooms. They appeared unoccupied. I stepped quietly in, closing the door behind me.

The house smelled of wax and new carpet. Under my feet, a flawless Aubusson padded dark oak. Above the wainscoting, cream wallpaper was dotted with tiny green flowers. The trim around the doors was a matching green. Windows were hung with reverse-pattern curtains. Antique tables displayed china washbowls.

I wouldn't have guessed Gretchen's taste was so Old World. Maybe the deviance of her previous life-style had nurtured an appreciation for the traditional.

It made me uncomfortable. I felt as if I were in a maiden aunt's house, and I had to be careful not to make a mess.

The carpet absorbed the sound of my footfalls. I crossed to the room on my left. It was a sitting room with an antique settee and a large oak secretary. Magazines were fanned over a malachite table.

I continued down the hall. The next room was lined with books, floor to ceiling. Two leather wing chairs shared an ottoman. A pile of books tottered beside one. The topmost was titled *Quantum Reality*.

At the end of the hall was an old-fashioned tiled kitchen. The sink was clear of dishes. A garbage pail showed take-out Chinese cartons.

I backtracked to the stairs. An anchored runner muffled my ascent.

I tried to quiet my breathing. If Gretchen was in, I would find her up here. I began rehearsing what I would say to her.

The stairs ended at another, shorter corridor. All the doors were open except one. I stopped and listened. I thought I heard a faint mewling, possibly a woman crying. I almost turned around. Bad enough to intrude. Worse to break in while she was crying.

I forced myself on. I stopped in front of the first room. A suitcase-sized metal oblong was mounted on a sturdy tripod. It faced a square foot of translucent plastic, possibly film, clamped into a vise grip. A few feet beyond that, another vise held a mirror. A second mirror was erected several feet away. Two video cameras lay beside a scatter of notebooks and pamphlets. One was titled *Holography in Cyberspace*.

The next room was full of computer and video equipment, much of it in labeled cartons. Some I'd seen before at Brother Mike's. Some was unfamiliar—rectangles studded with buttons and slots, metal gloves and helmets with wires and LCD readouts attached.

One thing was certain: Brother Mike had been staying here. From the look of it, he stayed here often.

Two other minuscule rooms contained beds. One bed was disheveled, the floor around it littered with what looked like professional journals. The other was buried under frilly comforters and shams.

I stared at it a long time. I stared because it was the only thing left to do before trying the remaining door. I didn't know whether to knock on that door or simply enter. I couldn't recapture the urgency that had persuaded me to break in.

In the end, I almost knocked and announced myself.

But I remembered the dead women in the theater; I forced myself to exercise caution rather than manners. I pushed the door slightly and slowly. I peered through the crack.

I was so shocked by what I saw, I almost rushed in. But Sandy Arkelett, silver-taped to a chair, shook his head to warn me back.

I swallowed my gasp; looked at him more carefully. He'd gotten my first message, perhaps—come here to find me. And he'd ended up secured to an oak chair with what looked like yards of duct tape. His hair spilled over his forehead and his nose twitched as if he longed to scratch it.

His eyes shifted back to something that was out of my line of sight. Probably to whomever had done this.

I'd noticed a telephone on the hall table. I didn't wait to find out who else was in the room. I backtracked. I picked up the phone, my hand over the earpiece to muffle the dial tone. I could again hear crying from the bedroom. Was it Gretchen? Was she taped, too?

I dialed 911.

The woman stopped crying. Her words seemed superhumanly loud after all my tiptoeing and breath-catching.

"What's that?" the voice demanded. "I closed that door. Didn't I close that door?"

I pressed the receiver to my ear. Once the dispatcher answered, the 911 computer would display the number and address here. If I could stay on the line long enough for one busy operator to pick up the phone—

At that moment, Margaret Lenin flew into the corridor.

Her hair was stringy and straight; she obviously hadn't taken time to curl it. Her face was streaked with tears. Mascara dappled her cheeks.

She rushed at me, clubbing me with a hard object. I dropped the phone, shielding myself with my forearms. She caught me on the cheek once; I felt an explosion of pain, hoped she hadn't splintered bone.

After the first shock, I tried to do more than defend myself. I tried to overpower her.

I heard Sandy shouting. I stopped when my brain finally made sense of his words: "Don't fight, Laura."

It was all I could do to obey. I wanted to fight; my body was shaking with adrenaline. But Sandy knew the situation better than I did. I trusted him.

I raised my hands in surrender.

In the scuffle, the phone had been pulled from its jack. I didn't know if I'd been on long enough for 911 to answer, long enough for the computer to display Gretchen's address. At best, assistance might be a long time coming.

"Margaret, please," I panted. "I came to help you. Remember the night you called me? I said I wanted to help. I still do."

"I didn't want you to pick me up. All you did was keep saying you were going to pick me up."

"Why did you call me, then?"

"You knew the situation. I didn't know who else to call." Looking suddenly guilty, she glanced at the object in her hand.

What I had feared, what I had assumed was a gun, turned out to be a metal tape dispenser.

Margaret? Had Margaret secured those women to their chairs? Or had she gone into the theater after they'd been bound, picking up the duct tape then?

I wanted to believe Sandy was right about the Women's Media Project. I envisioned them trooping into the theater like teachers to Babylon, trussing workers to their seats to force them to listen. (As if that could be persuasive; as if that could compete with "inspiration.")

Because I didn't want to believe Margaret had gone there with a gun and a tape dispenser to kill six women. Premeditation didn't explain her phone call to me.

"Did you get that tape from the Women's Media Project, Margaret? Did you walk in while they were making the women watch their show?"

She pushed hair off her damp face. "The Media Project show? The slides of magazine ads and all that? I was involved in that years ago; I used to go around and give that lecture. A lot of us did, especially women who felt conflicted. A lot of the sex-positive people came out of the Media Project. We came to terms with our sexuality and understood what real radicalism means. Reclaiming erotica instead of fighting it." But she didn't sound convinced.

"It's complicated." I tried to soothe. "No matter how you feel about the issue in the abstract, it gets complicated when it comes to your own sexual feelings."

"Arabella and Gretchen and a lot of people feel our thinking has evolved since the anti-porn days, but I'm not so sure." She straightened her spine, looking almost like the competent bank lawyer I'd once known. "I'm not so sure we didn't just buy into using each other the way men used to use us. We couldn't bear the portrayals of us, so we became that way, do you know what I mean? All that we're-so-hot-to-trot stuff. It used to be we knew it was a construct so men would feel okay about objectifying us. Now we're supposed to really feel that way. As a political statement."

There was supplication in her tone—she needed agreement. There was also anger. I didn't know what that meant.

"It's complicated, Margaret," I repeated, playing it safe. "If you think something's true, then it is true for you. You can't blame people for fooling themselves. People do it to survive. Or at least to feel okay about how they make their money."

Margaret looked puzzled. "When I belonged to the group, we used to say it was wrong to harass sisters—that our focus was male-dominated media. But I don't agree with that anymore. Women need to take responsibility for objectifying themselves and other women. They need to answer for what they do to each other. Especially lesbians. It's like the song 'Universal Soldier.' It can't happen without us, and we have to start blaming each other. It's dishonest to exempt ourselves. Because if we do, we end up screwing each other, and buying into getting screwed."

I imagined this view would play badly to immobilized women. Being forced into powerless haranguing at the end of a workday would be hell.

But if the Media Project had taped the women, why hadn't they untied them when they left? Had they known the janitor was due at three? Had they counted on a boyfriend coming soon to pick someone up? They'd left Hover handcuffed, trusting some minion would eventually free him.

I didn't want to think about the taped-over faces. I doubted the Media Project had done that. Their object had been to educate, albeit punitively.

But I couldn't push the thought away: Margaret was the one who'd resented Arabella's beautiful "fuck buddies." Maybe she'd remained there when the Media Project women left. Remained in disheartened jealousy of their beauty. Maybe all she'd wanted was to cover her "competition's" faces.

Maybe she hadn't realized it would kill them. She'd sounded crazy on the phone; at her wit's end, out of touch with reality. Surely a jury would sympathize; would take into account that her mother had been insane.

"Let me get you out of this, Margaret. There's a lawyer called Pat Frankel, she's right across the hall from me. A criminal lawyer in Dennis Heyerdahl's firm." I wished I could represent Margaret, but I'd have to be a witness, probably for the prosecution. "Let us get you out of the trouble you're in."

She giggled. "Oh, gosh. You don't even know the trouble I'm in."

She backed toward the door. Behind her, inside the room, Sandy was squirming, presumably to loosen the tape binding him to the chair. I knew it wouldn't work. If six women in a panic of suffocation hadn't been able to get free, neither would he.

Margaret pushed the door open farther.

30

AS SOON AS the door swung open, Sandy's cry made sense to me. There would have been little purpose in fighting Margaret. I might have gotten hurt. And it was no use hurting her. Because it wasn't Margaret who'd bound Sandy. It wasn't Margaret who sat nonchalantly pointing a gun at Gretchen.

As the door swung open, I watched Arabella de Janeiro turn the gun toward me.

"Hi," she said.

I heard myself reply, with disconcerting normalcy, "Hi."

"I'm awfully sorry." She sounded fretful. "I'm just trying to figure out what to do. Of all the times for a million people to drop by."

Her hair was tousled, rich with red-brown highlights. Her cheek and jaw and the skin around one eye showed a swollen mottling of greens and purples. She wore a tight white sweater, a short red skirt, and cowboy boots. Even slumped and splay-kneed, with bruises on her face, she looked like the box of some porn video. I couldn't decide if it was her extraordinary figure or merely its packaging. She might have been posed under the title *Debbie Gets Desperate*. "I really need to see Mike."

Gretchen sat on a foam mat, glancing at me only briefly. She watched Arabella, her lips in a grim line.

I didn't know what to say, what to make of it. "What are you do-ing?"

"Thinking, I guess," Arabella replied. "Waiting for him. He knows how they died; I know he does. *He* won't say." She nodded toward Sandy. "But Mike knows. I can feel it."

"You can wait for Mike without the gun," Gretchen said gently.

"Oh, right. I heard what he"—again she gestured toward Sandy—"said to you downstairs. That you should call the cops. That they don't trust me."

What was she afraid of? What did she think Sandy would tell the police if she let him go? He knew less than I did—or so I'd thought.

"You've been beaten and traumatized," I pointed out. "You're not thinking clearly. Sandy can't hurt you. And Gretchen's told you you're free to wait here."

"Yeah, well, maybe you don't know everything." She grabbed a crownful of her hair, scrunching it as if to ensure it didn't lie flat. "Maybe they won't let Mike see me—maybe they'll warn him. You don't know how Gretchen is. Mother hen. Number-one wife."

Gretchen sounded weary. "I've told you and told you. If Mike meets someone interesting in Silicon Valley, he could be gone for days."

"But you don't know that's where he went."

"No, I don't. But come on. He's been out of the area for a while. Of course he's going to go play with computers."

"He's still got some in boxes," Arabella pointed out. "In the other room. I saw them."

"But those are the ones he has." Gretchen's tone was patient. "He'll want to play with ones he doesn't have."

Arabella's chin quivered as if she might cry. She held a gun; I tried to think of her as dangerous.

But I didn't feel it. I didn't feel hostility, or even the kind of crazy energy I felt from Margaret.

"Why did you tape Sandy up? He doesn't mean you any harm," I repeated.

"He'll do something—he'll turn me in. I won't be able to wait for Mike."

Turn me in. I finally understood: this was an admission of guilt. "Turn you in for what? For taping the women in the theater?"

Out of the corner of my eye, I saw Gretchen shake her head.

"What do you mean, 'taping'? Videotaping?" There was a quality in her voice, a practiced ingenuousness, that reminded me of the sexy little pout plied by The Back Door sex workers. The question contained too much eroticized infantilism to sound genuine.

Behind me, Margaret laughed.

I caught my breath. If Margaret had indeed taken mad advantage of a situation created by the Women's Media Project, would she laugh about it? If she'd taped the women's faces, could she really laugh?

I shifted slightly, so that Margaret was in my peripheral vision. I didn't want to turn away from Arabella's gun.

"Those six dancers died of suffocation," I said. "I doubt if Mike knows that. But if you put the gun down, I'll give you details."

I heard Sandy's muttered protest. He believed the police plan was a sound one: wait for Arabella to blurt out something she shouldn't know.

But she might never do that. And telling her the truth seemed the quickest way to free Sandy.

"Don't be silly." Arabella looked annoyed. "How could they suffocate?"

Again Margaret giggled. I glanced at her. Then stared in open surprise. She looked radiant.

I'd worked with her on several debt-collection cases. She was a smart woman. A garden-variety yuppie, I'd have said before learning of her video.

What did her laughter mean? I'd hoped she hadn't understood

the consequences of her action—assuming she'd taped the women's faces. Now I wasn't sure.

"Let it go, Laura," Sandy begged. "Would you please not do this?"

The loud caw of a door buzzer startled me. Arabella gasped. She jerked the gun toward the front wall as if to take aim at the front door, a story below.

"Who now?" she demanded. "Who's that?"

I noticed she was shaking. She stood creakily, her free hand going to her ribs. An abrupt intake of breath betrayed her pain.

The rest of us remained in place as the buzzer rang again, several times sharply. She looked out the window.

"Oh, shit!" She stood there, gun dangling for an instant. Before I could persuade myself to lunge for it, she turned, aiming at me. "It's the police. Did you call them?"

"No."

"I saw you on the phone."

"I was calling my office. I didn't get through. Margaret interrupted." It was a quick lie, one I hoped wouldn't get me into trouble.

The buzzer rang again and again, accompanied by pounding. Thank God for 911's computer.

"You did call them!" Arabella handed Margaret the gun. "Take this. You've got to keep everyone up here." She grabbed Margaret's arm, aiming the gun at Sandy. "Just keep it pointed. Don't blow this, Margaret."

Margaret nodded, stepping closer to Sandy.

"Good. Stand close and keep it steady on him. They won't try anything if you keep it on him."

A shout rose from downstairs, the police either announcing their presence or threatening to beat the door in.

Arabella winced as she crossed the room.

Margaret stood inches from Sandy. Arabella had been smart to position her there. As high-strung as she was and as close as she was, rushing her would be risky. She could pull the trigger without even intending to.

I edged closer to the window.

Gretchen rose from her tailor's squat. "Margaret," she said, with a quick glance at me, "what's going on?"

Margaret, focused on her, didn't notice me sidling toward the window.

Below, we heard the front door open.

The window was directly above it. I was close enough to hear Arabella exclaim, "I'm so sorry! I was having trouble with my boyfriend, but he's gone now."

"Get away from there!" Margaret insisted. "And you sit back down."

I could hear the rumble of male voices.

Arabella's voice, higher in pitch, floated to me. "He's gone now. I'm sorry I bothered you. But he's gone now."

I held my breath, hoping to make out what they said next. Surely they'd investigate further? Surely they'd be suspicious of lies, even from a beautiful, sweet-voiced woman?

When I heard the door close, I felt my shoulder muscles knot.

A moment later, Arabella returned. Alone.

She crossed to me, lips pinched in rage. I thought she was going to strike me. Instead, she began to shake. She turned away, taking the gun from Margaret.

"She called nine-one-one," Arabella told her. "But I got rid of them."

"We'll have to tape her," Margaret said.

I backed closer to the window. My horror of restriction overrode every other emotion: I wouldn't let them tape me. No matter what.

Especially after having seen the women at the theater. There was no way I'd let myself be bound. Not when that might happen to me.

I glanced frantically over my shoulder, as if the window offered egress. I noticed a man down at street level, jaywalking toward the house.

With little visual detail upon which to rely, I trusted it was Brother Mike. The man was heading this way, and Hover was expected.

If he'd arrived before the police, I'd have trusted him to defuse the situation. But I'd changed the dynamic. Arabella had been sure from the outset that Sandy—and I, by extension—could incriminate her. And I'd inadvertently compounded her fear by calling 911. She might not let us go just because Hover walked in. She might sequester him, too.

I had to warn him. I had to alert him to call the police. If I could just get the timing right.

He would be on the sidewalk now, climbing the steps . . . how? At a bound? Slowly?

He'd open the door and shut it. Quietly? Or would he bang it?

I took no chances. At what I judged to be the proper moment, I slammed my fist against the window frame. "No!" I said. I pounded a few more times. "I won't be tied up. I want to know what this is about." Another thump in case Brother Mike had dawdled.

Surely he was inside by now. If I could alert him before Arabella became aware of his presence, we might stand a chance. He was supposed to be in tune with our "energies," wasn't he?

I had little experience with being telepathic, but I tried. I also raised my voice. "I won't be tied up! I don't understand why you're holding us at gunpoint. I don't understand what this is about. Margaret! For God's sake." I wasn't much good at creative ranting. "You're a bank lawyer!"

Arabella scowled at me. "Shut up! Just—"

"Wait a minute, wait a minute." Margaret looked flustered. "She doesn't get upset." She turned to Arabella. "Laura doesn't get upset."

"Calm down, everyone," Gretchen begged. "Laura, why don't you sit—"

"Of course I get upset!" I said, and meant it.

"Something's not right." Margaret began to look around the room. "She's talking so loud."

"Everybody, please," Gretchen pleaded, eyes on the gun. "Chill out."

I thought I heard a creaking in the corridor. I wished the door were fully, rather than partially, closed. But so far, Arabella and Margaret had their backs to it. And in spite of Margaret's insight, the two women remained focused on me.

"Of course I get upset when someone points a gun at me." I all but shouted the word "gun." "I get upset when someone tapes my partner to a chair. Especially when six people were murdered that way."

I hoped Brother Mike was in the hallway. I hoped he understood.

"You keep talking about getting murdered by being taped." Arabella's voice rose in pitch. "What are you talking about? All we did was tie them—" She stopped, looking rattled. Then grim.

"Something's wrong," Margaret insisted. "She's not acting like herself."

"What's she talking about? About the suffocating? Margaret? Do you know?" Arabella extended the arm holding the gun as if to stress she still meant business. She did a slow sweep, aiming at each of us in turn, settling finally for Sandy, in his ashen helplessness. "Margaret? Why is she saying that about the women? They didn't die taped up?"

"I don't know!" But it sounded like a childish lie. "I told you that."

Arabella squinted at her sometime lover. "All we did—" She closed her lips tight.

The lawyer in me applauded. Offer no detail; it can only be used against you.

All we did . . . was tie the women up?

Had it been she and Margaret who'd taped the women to their chairs?

Alongside the Women's Media Project? Or the two of them on their own, for reasons of their own?

But Arabella seemed genuinely confused by the references to suffocation. Did she think the women had been left alive, duct-taped to chairs? Didn't she realize they would suffocate with their airways covered?

Or had their faces still been exposed when she left? Had Margaret gone back later, after dropping Arabella at the hospital, with the tape remnants?

"Gretchen says it's part of the Hollywood formula to kill sex workers," I rambled. "Because they don't count as real people. But it's funny how I keep talking about six people dead when it's really seven."

"What are you going on about?" Arabella's pitch climbed to a near shriek.

"At The Back Door. Six women suffocated because their faces were completely taped over. And a man—"

I stopped when Arabella's mouth widened to a horrified circle. Her breath became audible, a chugging hyperventilation.

"A man in the corridor was killed, too. He was shot. And I'm treating him like a nonperson. I keep talking about the women, about six people. When it was really seven."

The blood had drained from Arabella's face. She was eerily still, in a rigor of shock. "Margaret?" she said. "What's she talking about?"

I glanced at Sandy. A glaze of sweat covered his face. His hair clung damply to his forehead. He watched Arabella.

"I don't know. How should I know?" Margaret backed away from her, tears brimming in her eyes.

She'd been a relatively undynamic lawyer, merely smart, merely good enough, with the usual wardrobe and refinements. I watched her now, reminded of television interviews of dumbfounded neighbors insisting serial killers had seemed so "regular."

Whatever Arabella's purpose in taping up her coworkers, she'd apparently meant to leave it at that. She'd apparently meant to walk away from their squirming anger.

She hadn't counted on her lover's jealousy exploding into a last-minute fit of cruelty.

"Or was it just because they were so beautiful?" I asked Margaret. "Were you just covering up their beauty?"

"Making everyone equal." She pinched her sweater. It took me a second to realize she was pinching her nipples. "Without implants." Not a half second later, in a firmer voice: "I have no idea what you're talking about."

Arabella's eyelids drooped. Her gun arm went down.

I could see Gretchen moving slowly forward. She looked almost feline in her focus on the gun.

But Arabella took a resolute step backward, shaking herself out of her stupor.

"Tape them up," she said curtly. "Margaret, do it."

"We're not going to hurt you," Gretchen soothed her. "The only person in here big and strong enough to hurt you is already taped, Arabella. Just calm down. We're not a threat to you. We're just waiting together for Brother Mike. Like we've done a hundred times."

Arabella was blinking rapidly, taking shallow breaths, the color flooding back to her bruise-mottled face. "No, tape them, tape them. I need time to think."

"That's right: don't trust them," Margaret urged. "They don't care about you." But she didn't seem to be talking about us. The pleading in her voice seemed of long standing and about something at the heart of their relationship.

"Oh, for goodness' sake!" Perhaps without meaning to, Arabella swung the gun toward Margaret. "Don't get flippy on me, Margaret. You don't own people, you spend time with them."

Margaret, who'd been reaching for a roll of silver cloth tape, stopped. She turned, vexation twisting her lips. "That's very naive. That's very self-serving."

I struggled to understand their argument, to exploit it. Were they talking about promiscuity? Jealousy?

"You were there for Arabella on her terms," I offered. I hoped I'd guessed right. I hoped they were talking about Arabella's relationship with her coworkers.

It felt a little sick pandering to Margaret's resentment. Maybe because I'd spent the last year accepting my lover's terms.

"Laura." Sandy's voice was vibrant with anger. Tied helplessly to a chair, he was the most vulnerable. He had the most to lose in my gamble.

But he didn't know Mike Hover was in the house; that by now—surely—Hover had heard the discussion and realized he must call the police. In the meantime, the more engaged Margaret remained, the less likely she'd tape me and Gretchen to chairs.

And, my claustrophobia aside, it might become essential to retain my freedom of movement. Who knew what might happen before help arrived?

"That's right," Margaret said. Her words were thick with emotion, almost slurred. "I did it your way because I wanted to grow. I wanted to love you exactly as you are." She reached a shaky hand toward Arabella.

Arabella began to weep. "What did you do to my friends?"

Margaret looked like she'd been slapped. "Friends? They beat you up! Those women had you beaten up!"

I felt my flesh chill. Arabella's coworkers had done that to her? Why?

"Shut up! Shut up!" She tried to keep sobs from racking her bruised body.

"You told me all the time how *they* were your buddies, and you fuck your buddies for a living, and that's so cool and nineties and sex-positive and all that. And I have to pretend there's this bogus line: sex on one side and emotions on the other. I've got to do all this work to feel okay about these supposed buddies of yours—who could be anyone that gets hired off the street, with herpes or AIDS or whatever. And I'm supposed to be turned on by you putting your fingers and your tongue in them, just like one of those wives in the porn movies or the slicks. I'm supposed to buy into not only what turns on the creeps that go to the shows, but all this *On Our Backs* sex-positive, political-in-quotes stuff that doesn't look any different from the *Playboy* mansion bullshit." Margaret was red-faced, waving pleading hands at Arabella. "You never let me tell you how hard it was for me. You always made me pretend that it wasn't. But it was."

Arabella had swallowed her sobs. She stood rigid, gun closer to her body, wavering a bit in its aim. "It's my job. And I like it. It's my life. And you knew that going in."

Damn. Had I hallucinated Brother Mike's crossing the street toward the house? Had I imagined the creak of oiled boards in the hall?

Where was he? Where were the police he should have called by now?

In a strangled voice, Margaret concluded, "I knew what? That your fuck buddies, your so-called friends, were going to hire someone to beat you up? And why? Just for giving Brother Mike your home movies."

Her home movies? Movies of herself and her "buddies"? Having sex? Practicing their acts?

I supposed Brother Mike rejoiced to have the footage. He could only reimage film to which he held the copyright. He could only use images he'd captured himself or which had been given to him for his use.

But the women at The Back Door might not have appreciated having videos of them made available to him. He'd used them for financial gain, to improve his devotees' bodies by "morphing" them with more commercially acceptable ones. And those women made a living selling their images. Arabella had given away the thing they sold. She'd told them her home videos were for her personal scrapbook, and then she'd turned them over to her guru.

They must have noticed parts of themselves in his newly released videos.

"Your coworkers hired the men to beat you up." I tried to make my tone sympathetic, soothing. "That must have really hurt you."

Arabella shook her head. Tight-lipped and tear-streaked, she seemed determined to look tough. "He wasn't using the films the

way they thought. Sure, he was making money, but he wasn't doing it for himself; he wasn't doing it to get rich off our bodies. The
money was going for something totally outside the industry. He was
buying the future."

"How brutal of them. To have you physically hurt." She might
as well have had a mean pimp.

"They thought it would be like this token thing, this little lesson
they'd teach me. Like they were being so alternative: not getting a
lawyer or going to the cops or creating a fuss or whatever. Like they
were just making a point. They knew I'd find out—all I had to do
was pay the guys who beat me up. That's all I had to do. It took me
about one hour to find them and buy the information. Because I
was supposed to find out. That was the whole point." Her voice was
flat with fury. "Except everybody knows how easy I bruise. And that
means time off work. And they really hurt me. Maybe they got carried away, like the women said. But even so, it wasn't fair. Because
Mike's not in the industry. The videos were for something else. So
I fucking hit them back. They deserved it."

Their faces had been taped over. And so I had seen only blank
silver masks. I hadn't seen anything to reveal the women had been
hit.

Except for the trickle of blood on one of their necks. I had noticed that, certainly. But in my horror, I hadn't considered what it
might mean.

"You took Margaret to the theater so you'd have an assistant,
someone to tape the women up for you." I heard Sandy groan. Never
upset a person with a gun; that must be what he was thinking. But
he hadn't found the dead women. His dreams wouldn't be haunted
by the tableau, made grislier now that I knew more facts.

Arabella had held the gun while Margaret taped the women. She'd
handed the gun to Margaret while she hit them, while she squared
things. Perhaps she and Margaret had arrived in separate cars, and
she'd left first, going back to the hospital as her pain increased. Or

maybe Margaret had driven Arabella there, returning afterward. One way or the other, Margaret had ended up alone in the theater with the six girded women.

And, sick with frustration and jealousy, she had covered the lovely faces of her rivals.

She'd told me some of this on the phone that night. She'd told me Arabella had called her. *Why* had she called? Margaret had tearfully asked.

I hadn't reached the theater soon enough to keep Margaret from acting on her pain. But, unlike her mother, she hadn't killed herself. She'd killed the other woman. All six of them.

And the man who'd kicked the door in must have scared her, must have panicked her as she was leaving the theater. In all likelihood, the gun Arabella held now was the one she'd left with Margaret that night. In all likelihood, it was the weapon Margaret had used to kill the unlucky boyfriend.

"I trusted you." Arabella spoke through clenched teeth. Her face was a study in restraint. "I was so upset. So grateful to you for helping."

"My baby," Margaret said fondly. "You needed to go get looked after. I made you go back to the hospital. And I was right, wasn't I?"

"You told me you were going to undo them. But you taped their faces up." Arabella's tone said, Please contradict me. "Didn't you know that would suffocate them?"

God, I wished Brother Mike would do something. I wished the cops would come soon.

"When my mother went for her walk, she left me in the car. Did you know that?" Margaret's face was turned sideways, like a bird's. "I got heatstroke waiting for her to come back. I almost died from it."

I noticed Gretchen edging closer to Arabella. Arabella didn't seem to notice, her attention fully on Margaret.

"But she didn't mean it," Margaret continued. "It didn't have anything to do with me. It was about something else."

In taping the faces, Margaret had tried to cover the source of her pain. At least, I hoped that's how her lawyer would paint it to the jury.

I repeated what I'd said to her earlier. "I can help you, Margaret. We can get you out of this."

"You made my life hell with your fucking whimpering jealousy." The sudden hatred in Arabella's voice stunned me. "Now you've killed my friends."

"They beat you up," Margaret wailed. "My lovey."

"I took care of that, Margaret. I got back at them. I'd have been fine with going right back to work with them. And they'd have been fine with it, too. *They* understood me."

Suddenly, as Gretchen surged forward to stop it, the situation spun out of control.

Gretchen lunged for Arabella's arm. And Arabella shifted, took aim, and shot Margaret dead.

Right in front of me. In a way, because of me. In a way I might never come to terms with, because of me.

An instant after the shot was fired, Gretchen was on top of Arabella.

Arabella, bruised and crazy with her sudden knowledge, was no match for Gretchen. She let go of the gun. She lay there without fighting, without squirming.

Sandy bounced his chair closer and kicked the gun across the room.

I just stood there, looking at Margaret, collapsed at my feet, half her face a pulp of shattered tissue and bone, her eyes open and cold as marbles, pieces of blown-back tissue stuck to the pupils.

I stood there, listening to Sandy shout, "You motherfucker. You stupid heartless egotistical motherfucker."

It took me a few seconds to make sense of the words. And then they lanced me. Because they were—and they weren't—true.

I had caused this. I couldn't deny it.

But I hadn't meant to. I'd been stalling. I hadn't wanted to end up bound like those women. I'd been buying time. That's all. Never meaning to cause this.

I looked at him. My pain was all the more acute because I knew, after years of putting the knowledge aside because it didn't fit my life and the pattern of my mistakes, that I loved him. Sandy was my one real friend.

He'd called me an egotistical motherfucker. And he was right. And wrong, too.

I looked at him, and found he wasn't looking at me.

I looked at him, his nostrils flared with fury, madly bouncing his chair toward the door, and found him staring into the corridor, staring at a spot he could see but I couldn't.

When he bounced close enough to the door, he repeated, "You motherfucker!" and he kicked it.

It swung open. Brother Mike stood there, a video camera in his hand.

I had stalled, waiting for Mike Hover to call the police. Waiting for him to come in and soothe his devotees. To change the situation. To fix things somehow.

Instead, he'd heard my words and seen an opportunity. He'd gone to his room and gotten his video camera.

He'd collected more images for his computer experiments. Exciting images, certainly.

He'd be able to reimage a murder now. He could splice in naked women, color in auras, make holographic history, perhaps. Without fear of copyright infringement.

He stood in the corridor, camera hanging from his limp arm. He stared at Sandy and shook his head, backing away from the bucking chair and the flood of enraged curses.

"I'd have come in in a minute," he swore. "I'd have come in and helped in just a minute."

I looked again at Margaret, at the horrible pulp she'd become. I looked at Gretchen, cradling Arabella to comfort her. Arabella was keening, curled into a fetal position.

She'd tried to get revenge on her "friends," and things had gone hideously and fatally awry. In great stress—stress I'd fueled—she'd killed her lover. And I supposed she was realizing now that eight people were dead. That her life was changed forever.

Perhaps Brother Mike, psychically tuned to our "energies," had felt it coming.

But he'd chosen to delay, to let us play chicken. He'd chosen his goal—his light show of technological progress—over the immediate, perilous reality of the situation.

He'd used his devotees again. Their images—their contribution to technology's future—had been more important to him than anything else. Again.

Arabella had been right about that.

In a time of painful need, she'd come here to find her guru. To do to him what she'd done to her coworkers? Or to receive comfort and absolution from him?

Sandy shouted at me to cut him free. His chair cracked fiercely against the doorframe. But his frenzy was too ungoverned to get him through, to get him into the corridor to do whatever it was he wanted to do to Brother Mike.

I knelt beside Margaret, looking up at Michael Hover. His eyes met mine.

He said, "I almost had enough. It can make you blind, going for that last little bit."

I knew, without flattering myself that it was a premonition, that no jury would understand. No jury would fathom his lust to own images, his belief that changing them would catapult us into an epoch of brilliant knowledge.

A jury would see a man who'd allowed his own devotees—people he could easily sway, easily save—to smolder into explosion.

A jury would see other gurus, men who'd cavalierly stripped the wealth and sense and "natural" sexual modesty from their followers. They would see Jim Jones and Rajneesh.

And, in a way, they'd be right.

I listened to Sandy's stream of invective, his demands that I unbind him so that he could act out his rage. I listened to Gretchen, whimpering as she held Arabella; Gretchen, so miserable with her deadening career she'd reached out for spiritual stimulation.

Brother Mike had used her, yes. But that had been her decision; she'd wanted to believe. Like the women at The Back Door, she'd selected her perspective. And I, with my history of bad choices, who was I to judge?

"I wanted to help you, Margaret," I heard myself whisper. "Truly."

Still looking at Michael Hover, I commanded, "Don't say anything else. You need a criminal lawyer." Over Sandy's infuriated cry, I added, "You, too, Arabella, please. Don't say anything. Wait for your lawyer."

Perhaps Sandy could justify his wrath: he'd embraced unequivocal values his whole life. He'd been able to dislike Hal, to dismiss Ted McGuin, as if reality weren't layered, as if people weren't complicated. But in a way, I'd killed Margaret and in a way I hadn't.

Who the hell was I to judge anybody?

I'd call the police. I'd keep warning Mike Hover and Arabella de Janeiro to remain silent. Just as I'd remain silent about having discovered those seven dead—and still, to my shame, anonymous—people.

And I would wait a little longer to unbind Sandy.

Maybe in a while he'd understand. Maybe in a while he'd forgive me. For not untying him sooner, and for my complicity.

I spoke again to Margaret's lifeless half a face. "I'm so sorry. I thought it would go differently. I thought someone would intervene." But we were alone in life, hadn't I been telling myself that all month?

Sandy shouted at me to untape him. Threatened to push Hover's head through a wall.

Blaming him totally so he wouldn't have to blame me?

I rose and walked to the door. I'd call 911 before undoing Sandy. I'd wait until he calmed down.

As I threaded past his chair, I turned and touched his face. I watched his anger fade to concern, to a beseeching, searching sympathy. It was like ice on a burning wound.

I was lucky to have a friend, not a master, not a guru, not a needy, crazy lover insisting I ignore my own wishes.

I was lucky to have Sandy. Life had been arid without his friendship.

"You can untie me now," he said. "I hear you."